BEARS ON THE ROAD
TO DAMASCUS

BEARS ON THE ROAD TO DAMASCUS

A COLLECTION OF STORIES BY

PATRICK ROONEY

iUniverse, Inc.
Bloomington

BEARS ON THE ROAD TO DAMASCUS
A Collection of Stories

iUniverse books may be ordered through booksellers or by contacting:

iUniverse
1663 Liberty Drive
Bloomington, IN 47403
www.iuniverse.com
1-800-Authors (1-800-288-4677)

Cover design and illustration ©2012 Sarah E Melville, Sleeping Basilisk Design

ISBN: 978-1-4759-0674-5 (sc)
ISBN: 978-1-4759-0676-9 (hc)
ISBN: 978-1-4759-0675-2 (ebk)

Printed in the United States of America

iUniverse rev. date: 04/02/2012

For all my apartment 8 cohorts:
Sarah, Conor, Brandon, Peter, Blair and Kassondra.

INTRODUCTION

You hold in your hands a strange book. If I didn't know at first just how strange this book is, it became impossible to ignore after reading the editorial evaluation iUniverse was kind enough to provide. For the most part the evaluation liked all the stories on an individual basis, but expressed confusion over the fact that "there are at least four genres present in the work." This paragraph sums up the problem nicely:

> *Execution:* **Does the story have sufficient commercial pace and appeal or literary value?**
>
> A number of the "horror" stories are powerful and will appeal to readers of this genre. The fairy tales will also appeal, but to a very different audience—namely, children. The nonfiction will be of interest to a general adult audience. However, having all of these genres, plus a poem, in the same collection is problematic, especially because they have different audiences.

The most jarring example was a story included in the first draft called *Bitch*, which is a five-page story about a brainwashed sex slave and "uses language that will offend a majority of readers." So that's all well and good, but then what are a couple fairy tales doing in the same book?

> "'Elijah's Violin' seems out of place with the others. It is a gentle retelling of a traditional (apparently) tale of a fictional land, and it would fit better in a book of folk tales. Similarly, "Cyrus and the Dragon" is a fairy tale most appropriate for kids. It

does not fit with the harsh and brutal tales of rape and murder in the first part of the book."

What to do? I didn't have nearly enough material for four genre-specific books, and didn't feel like abandoning my current project to write them. I almost despaired, until I remembered that I'm self-publishing and can do whatever I want. I ditched *Bitch*, never having been totally comfortable with the idea of my mom reading it, anyway. Anyone who wants to read it should email me at shmatrick19 @ gmail.com, and I'll be happy to send you a copy.

Moving on, I'd like for you, the reader, to think of this book as a buffet. There are very different entreés available, and if you eat them all at once, they'll probably taste weird. But I hope you'll find something you like. Thanks for coming.

-Patrick

MENU

CYRUS AND THE DRAGON

This is a story from the land of Rane, a mysterious and magical place. The land of Rane is one of mountains and rivers, lakes and forests. The people of Rane live a peaceable existence, and many of the things that do not make sense to you did not make sense to them. For example, in the land of Rane there is no such thing as money, and the people would all laugh at you if you tried to explain to them why they would ever need it. In the land of Rane no person has any more power than anyone else, and the children are taught how to grow flowers and how to play drums with as much seriousness as they are taught grammar and history. In the land of Rane the roads are almost always just hard-packed dirt, and the untamed wilderness is always close by.

There was a boy who lived in the land of Rane whose name was Cyrus. Cyrus loved his mother and his father and his older sister Kim, but he felt that there was something missing in his life, and he thought he recognized what that something was when he went over to his friends' houses. His friend Conor had a pet rabbit, which was a little shy, but which was very soft when you finally got a hold of it. His friend Michelle had a big friendly dog and his friend Stephen had a slinky black cat. Cyrus got it into his head that he wanted a pet.

He wanted a pet dragon.

He went around his village and told everyone he knew that he was going to catch a dragon. The people of Rane all said the same thing: "What are you going to do when you find one?"

Finally one morning Cyrus decided that the time had come. He packed a knapsack with food and things he believed might be helpful in catching a dragon. "Mom," he said to his mom, "I'm going off to catch a dragon."

His mother turned a little watery in the eyes and said that she would be very worried about him, but that if this was something he really needed to do, he ought to go do it. "Just be *careful*," she said as she waved goodbye. "Find a *small* dragon."

Cyrus set off on a trail into the wilderness and kept on his way for days, crossing streams and rivers, and always keeping on the lookout for possible signs of dragons—a scorched rabbit skeleton, for instance.

One day he came upon a deep and wide canyon. He groaned to himself, for he had found no such indications that he was yet in dragon country, and the canyon was impossible to cross. To go around would likely take weeks or even months, for the canyon stretched as far as he could see in both directions.

"Oh, if I could only fly like the birds, this would be no obstacle!" Cyrus cried to a large hawk overhead.

To his surprise, the hawk flashed its red feathers, wheeled around in the air and touched down in front of him.

"Why do you wish to cross the canyon?" the hawk asked.

"I'm looking for a dragon," said Cyrus, "and I'm sure there must be one over the canyon."

"Hmm," said the hawk, ruffling its feathers. "I will carry you over the canyon . . . for a price."

"All right," said Cyrus. He noticed again just how deep the canyon was. It was a long way down.

"Do you have anything to eat?" asked the hawk.

Cyrus took off his knapsack and dug through it.

"I have peanuts," he said. The hawk shook its head, swiveling it quickly the way birds do. "Blueberry muffins . . ."

"That'll do," the hawk said. Cyrus handed the muffins his mother had baked to the hawk, who gobbled them up quick as a flash. "Get on my back," said the hawk. "And hold on tight to my feathers."

Cyrus climbed on, and the hawk leaped over the edge of the canyon. The boy felt its powerful wings rise and fall swiftly on either side of him as they soared above the abyss.

"Thank you, thank you, kind hawk," exclaimed Cyrus. "Now I am sure I will catch a dragon."

"Why," the hawk asked, "are you so obsessed with dragons?"

Cyrus had long ceased to object to the word "obsessed." "When I think about dragons, I am just so grateful that they exist," he said. "They are the ideal creatures. Powerful animals who have arms, legs, and wings, and who breathe fire! It doesn't get any better than that."

"Yet their wings are batlike," said the hawk. "And their bodies scaly. Anyway, hawks are much faster."

"Hoh, I doubt that," Cyrus said carelessly.

The hawk picked up its pace. Its pride was stung, and so it beat its wings faster and faster. Suddenly, the hawk made a tremendous zoom forward, just as a gust of wind from the opposite direction swept over them. Cyrus was blown off the hawk's back with a cry, clutching handfuls of feathers as he plummeted.

With despair Cyrus watched the bottom of the canyon rush towards him, and then he noticed that there was a river at its bottom. The only thing he could think of was to try very hard to keep his feet pointed straight towards the water.

He sliced into the cold water like a knife, and shot all the way to its dark floor, which he pushed firmly against with his feet. With a gasp he emerged at the surface and swam towards the river bank. He staggered onto the bank and collapsed onto the sand, trying to get his breath back and to stop his heart from racing.

He suddenly noticed there was someone watching him—a girl looking out at him from the window of a small house that stood alone by the river.

"That was quite a fall you took," she called. "Come on in and dry off."

He did, and found himself wrapped in a warm towel. He thanked the girl, who told him with a sad smile that it was no trouble at all. It was then that Cyrus first heard a baby crying, and she went to retrieve it from its crib in the corner, cradling it against her shoulder. She must have intended to comfort the child, but instead herself burst into tears.

"Miss," Cyrus asked the girl, "what is the matter? Why are you so sad?"

"I bear a sad tale," the girl told him. "My baby is ill and will surely—" she choked back a sob—"die by the end of the month unless it is provided a difficult cure. A kindly witch cast a spell which would save my child, but its conditions are near impossible! A person with a heart of gold must sacrifice five years from the end of his life, and then my child will himself live a full life. I would gladly offer this sacrifice myself—I'd give fifty years!—but the witch's limited magic dictates it must be a stranger who performs this rite."

"I'll do it," Cyrus said. "Five years is perhaps a lot to lose—that's half as old as I am now, and you could pack a lot of living into that time—but perhaps not so many compared to the entire life of your child."

As soon as Cyrus had spoken, the baby stopped its crying and began to gurgle and squeal with health and good cheer. The girl cried out and covered Cyrus with kisses.

"You, good and selfless boy! You have saved my child! Listen: I am a scholar of great distinction. I believe I can best repay you by imparting knowledge to you of any subject. What is it that you would like to learn above all else?"

Cyrus did not need to be asked twice. And so it was that the scholar provided him with everything he needed to know about where and how to catch a dragon. She pointed him towards the shadowy recesses of the canyon he had so recently been soaring above. "Dragons sleep in caves this time of afternoon," she told him.

Soon enough Cyrus found such a cave. It was dark and it was hard to tell how far it tunneled. It smelled like death. He heard with a thrill a low breathing coming from within. Instinctively he reached in his knapsack for a match, but they were all soaked and useless from his fall in the river. So Cyrus crept as softly as he could into the cave.

There was a dragon there. It was not fully grown yet, only about twenty feet long from head to tail. Cyrus stared at it, enthralled. It was even more beautiful than he had imagined. It was dark green, with a narrow head and tiny horns. It had a narrow body, though its shoulders and belly were large, and its four legs ended in sharp, hooked claws. Its wings were curled against its sides.

Suddenly the dragon opened its eyes, which were bright yellow, and, seeing the intruder, shot forth a ribbon of blue flame from its mouth. Cyrus dodged the fire, feeling the heat on the back of his neck as he quickly reached into his knapsack. He pulled out several pounds of raw beef, cut tri-tip style and slightly rancid. The dragon, poised to let loose another stream of fire, sniffed the air.

Cyrus tossed the meat as unthreateningly as he could towards the dragon, who chomped into it at once. When the dragon finished it, it licked its chops and burped a slightly uncomfortable-sounding burp, accompanied by a small green flame. Cyrus tossed a plum towards the dragon, which seemed to help settle its stomach. Then the dragon squinted suspiciously at the boy.

Cyrus pulled out a wooden flute from his knapsack. He shook the water out of it, and began to play the calmest, most soothing song he knew. The dragon, with its belly larger than it had been when Cyrus had first come upon it, snorted again. Cyrus watched its eyelids droop lower and lower until its low snores again echoed through the cave.

Cyrus continued to play the flute as he inched his way closer to the dragon. When he stood just next to it he reached out his hand and stroked the cool scaly skin. He looked closely at the dragon's scales on the back of its neck. All those who had ever successfully caught and befriended a dragon, the scholar told him, could read letters in the lines between the scales that no one else could. He ran his finger over a scale that seemed curved: he thought he saw an "R."

"Rork!" Cyrus said clearly. "Your name is Rork!"

The dragon awoke with a start and Cyrus continued to stroke its back. Then it rose to his feet and Cyrus drew back, frightened. The dragon extended his neck and nudged Cyrus's shoulder. Hesitantly, he reached out again to pet it. The dragon gave a soft growl that sounded as though it might communicate pleasure.

Slowly, slowly Cyrus raised one leg over the dragon's slender body, and brought it down on the other side. He held his breath, then settled his weight onto its back.

"Fly, Rork," he whispered.

With a terrific lunge, the dragon raced forward. As daylight exploded through the entrance of the cave, Rork swept enormous wings out from its body and beat them once, bringing them into the air like a kite, and then steadily pumping them as Cyrus clung securely to his dragon's sides. They spiraled through the air to the top of the canyon, and then soared back towards home, Cyrus's village in the land of Rane.

ELIJAH'S VIOLIN

Adapted from the Jewish folk tale

Once upon a time in the world of Nu, which is more magical and untamed than our own, there was a war. The forces of despair were pitted against humanity. The forces of despair had kidnapped the muse of music, and it was feared that they may even have killed it. Throughout all the lands, and all the kingdoms, music was lost. Drums made no sound, brass did not resonate, and reeds became still and unresponsive. Even the old woman who lived by the lake was unable to make music, either by her own voice or by any of the many instruments she knew how to play. This was sad, because the citizens of the Kingdom of Rane had grown accustomed to coming to hear her play more instruments than they had even thought existed.

It was rumored that the forces of despair planned to take poetry next, and so the kings of all the kingdoms resolved to go to battle. The king of Rane called his three daughters to him before he went off to fight and said: "I love you dearly, my daughters. If I should return victorious from this war, I should like to bring each of you a gift. Tell me, what would you like?"

The oldest daughter, whose name was Nicole, said, "Father, I would love for you to bring me back a diamond—a big one, and shaped like a star."

The second daughter, named Sarah, said, "Father, would you please bring me back a beautiful gown—woven from pure gold?"

But the youngest daughter, named Danielle, said, "Father, I would only desire that you return home safely from the war."

The king was touched at this and thanked his daughter. "But Danielle, because I love you, I'd like to bring you back a gift from my travels. Take a few days to think of anything you'd like."

Princess Danielle went to go sit by the lake near their palace to look into its blue waters and think.

"What's wrong, child?" a voice asked her. Danielle turned to see the old woman who lived by the lake standing before her. She wore a shawl, and had green eyes and purple eyebrows.

"I don't know what gift to ask of my father, the king," Danielle said.

The old woman nodded. "Ask him," she said, "for Elijah's violin."

"But you know, violins aren't working very well these days," said Danielle.

"Never mind that, child. Just ask for Elijah's violin. You must do this."

On the eve of the king's departure he sent for the youngest princess. "What gift have you decided on?" he asked her.

"I would like you to bring me Elijah's violin, please," said Danielle.

"Violins aren't working very well these days," the king said. But the princess repeated that this was what she desired, and so off to battle the king went.

As it turned out, the forces of humanity roundly defeated the enemy despair. Upon their victory, the troops in the field immediately attempted a song, but the muse of music was still missing. The king of Rane set out quickly to find his gifts for his daughters. A large diamond shaped like a star was quickly procured, and a dress made out of pure gold was tailored to fit Princess Sarah's exact measurements. But Elijah's violin proved more difficult to find.

So the king set out on a quest. He set sail, and scoured the four corners of the world, and at last was led to seek the advice of a wise old man who lived a hermit existence in a cave.

"Wise man," asked the king, "please give me advice as to where I might find Elijah's violin."

"Elijah's violin is in the possession of the king of Nehm," the old man said. He had green eyes and purple eyebrows. "In the days of the war, the forces of despair saw that his daughter, who would one day be ruler of Nehm, had a spirit for beauty and a voice for truth. Therefore they mysteriously turned her into stone—no one knows how. If you break that spell and free the princess, you will be richly rewarded."

The old man gave the king three long hairs. "These are from the bow of Elijah's violin," he said. "Burn them in the princess's presence and the spell will be broken."

The king was extremely grateful. "Thank you old man!" he cried. "How can I repay you for your generosity?"

"Don't worry about that," said the old man. "It is your daughter who will repay me by setting free the imprisoned melodies."

"Old man," said the King, puzzled. "Do you know my daughter? May I have the privilege of knowing your name?"

"My name is Elijah," said the old man, and at that he returned to the shadows of his cave and the king went on his way.

Soon the King of Rane reached the palace of Nehm, and upon gaining an audience with the king and queen announced his intention to cure their daughter.

"Very well," said the Queen of Nehm, "but we loath hacks and snake oil salesmen. For this reason, we have decreed that anyone who fails to cure Princess Scarf will have weights attached to his feet before he is hung from the ceiling by his ears. After being stretched in this way, the phony doctor will be squashed flat like a latke."

"That sounds reasonable," said the king, and went on to see the princess.

Princess Scarf seemed to be alive and dead at the same time, which startled the king badly. At first she appeared to be simply a statue of a princess, but with great effort she was able to speak.

"I do hope you will be able to help me, sir," she said, the head and lips of the statue moving suddenly.

"I will, my friend," said the king. "But tell me, how did you come to be turned into stone?"

The statue quivered and shook while the princess gathered up the energy to speak. She said: "I was looking into a mirror one day, one that I had never seen before. It was beautiful, with ornate designs and jewels in its frame. Suddenly as I looked into it, my image ceased to imitate me. I was filled with fear as the copy of my own face and body stepped through the mirror as though there were no boundary. It seized me, and thrust me back where it came from. I found myself on the other side of the mirror, just as though there was no glass at all, in the form in which you see me now." Then the statue was exhausted, and could speak no more.

"What an incredible story! Don't worry, I think this will do the trick," the king told her. He took out the hairs from the bow of Elijah's violin that the old man had given him, struck a match, and set them afire. The hairs were quickly reduced to ashes, and the princess's form become living flesh once more.

The royal family rejoiced at their daughter's return. The king told Princess Scarf that to defeat her doppelganger, she must first blindfold herself, and then smash the mirror from which the spirit had come.

"What inestimable assistance you have been to us!" the King of Nehm exclaimed. "You may have anything you like as a reward."

"I'd like Elijah's violin," the king said. The king and queen reminded him that violins weren't working very well lately, but he persuaded them that this truly was the reward he desired. And so at long last, the king had Elijah's violin, which was of unparalleled craftsmanship, and hundred of years old, and set off at once for home.

Upon his arrival the Princesses Nicole and Sarah exclaimed excitedly upon receiving their gifts, and at once ran off to their rooms to admire them. But Princess Danielle first embraced her father, and begged him to tell her all about his adventures.

After this, the king was tired from his journey and went to retire, so Danielle took the violin up to her room and put the bow to the strings.

At once, music came forth! It seemed to Danielle that the violin was almost playing itself, the way the bow moved effortlessly across the strings and her fingers nimbly crafted melodies she'd never heard before. And all around the kingdom of Rane and the whole world of Nu, people rejoiced at the return of music.

Now, it had been so long since Danielle had heard music, let alone played it, that she could have gone on playing for hours, or even days. But she was startled by the sudden appearance of a young man in her room.

"Why," she cried, "where did you come from?"

"I come from the Kingdom of Dae, far from here," he said. "I suddenly heard music—music!—and the next thing I knew I was transported from my palace all the way through your window. My name is Prince Nemi."

Well, Prince Nemi was handsome and knew a good joke or two. When he played a beautiful song on Elijah's violin, Danielle fell head-over-heels for him. And of course Nemi was already in love with the savior of music. For several weeks, Danielle had only to play Elijah's violin, and Nemi would arrive through their windows. Before long, they promised their hearts to each other and looked forward to their wedding. In this way often music is the path towards finding love.

There were only two people in the entire kingdom of Rane who were unhappy about the return of music: Princess Nicole and Princess Sarah. Now there were bands everywhere on the streets—musicians with questionable ideas and questionable behavior. It was all anybody could do to stay proper anymore.

One day the two older sisters heard noises coming from Danielle's room. They eavesdropped, and determined that a man visited Danielle through her window each time she played Elijah's violin. When their younger sister went out, the two snuck into her room. They joked cruelly about smashing the violin, but didn't quite dare. Instead, Nicole closed the window and Sarah broke the glass. Then Nicole picked up the violin and drew a screeching, mangled tune from it. When Prince Nemi arrived, he was cut badly by the broken glass on his face, arms and body, and disappeared.

When Danielle returned and saw her lover's blood on the broken glass, she knew at once what had happened and fled quickly to the old woman who lived by the lake for advice.

"Wipe your tears, dear," the old woman told her. "All is not lost. You must go to the kingdom of Dae. Once there, if the prince has bled quite a lot, you must burn three strings from Elijah's violin to cure him. This is strong magic, and so hairs from the bow will not suffice."

"Is there no other way?" asked the princess.

"Child, do not fear," said the old woman. "I'll make you new ones."

"Oh, thank you old woman!" Danielle said.

"One last thing—" the old woman said. "It can sometimes be useful to disguise yourself as a man." And she winked a green eye beneath her purple eyebrow.

And so the princess set off to rescue her prince. The geography in the world of Nu is very confused and inconsistent, and so as much as Danielle walked and walked and walked, she still found herself hopelessly lost, with no clear idea of whether she might be closer or farther away from Dae than she was in the first place.

At last she sat down to rest beneath a tree filled with chattering doves. She sought to catch an hour's rest, and so closed her eyes and leaned her head against the elder tree's sturdy trunk. Suddenly she heard voices talking:

"—prince all cut up and bleeding."

"I only wonder what he was up to to get himself in such—"

Danielle opened her eyes, but there was no one around except for the doves.

"Cooo. Cooo," said the doves. "Chirp."

Danielle closed her eyes again, only to hear the birds' chirping shift into speech the moment she couldn't see them.

"Hard to find the kingdom of Dae."

"Sure is, especially if you're not a bird."

"I have to admit, sometimes I feel *so* important being a bird—and guarding the map tree, too."

"If word got out about the leaves of our tree, the poor people of Dae would never get any privacy or rest."

"Chirp chirp chirp."

Danielle had opened her eyes once more and quickly plucked a leaf from the tree. To her amazement, the veins on the leaf clearly indicated how one could travel directly to Dae. Danielle set out at once, and reached the palace gates in no time.

Here she dressed herself in men's clothes, and went in to present herself as a doctor.

"We would love for you to cure our son," the King of Dae told Danielle, "but we must warn you that should you fail, weights will be attached to your legs before you are hung by your ears from the ceiling. As soon as you stretch from ceiling to floor, you will then be squashed flat as a latke." This was a popular punishment among royalty with afflicted offspring at the time.

"I am confident in my abilities," Danielle said in her gruffest, manliest voice. "I only ask to have privacy with the prince."

She was left alone with the prince and at once threw off her disguise. The sight of her love so cut up and bloody made her want to weep and throw herself upon him, but she resisted. She snapped three strings from Elijah's violin, and set them afire.

Instantly Prince Nemi sprang up, his wounds vanished without so much as a scar. "My love!" he exclaimed. The king and queen rushed into the room and were so overjoyed at their son's recovery that they insisted the two be married that very afternoon. The princess and the prince lived happily ever after and many were the times that the melodies of Elijah's violin were heard drifting over the land.

LEAVING THE BUNGALOW

Abbey Road was her favorite, but that didn't mean she couldn't enjoy the *White Album*. Events with any kind of stamina, like road trips or long, enjoyable weekends, often develop their own soundtracks, and Robin and Bill's Snowboarding Weekend Extravaganza, as Robin called it (with more and more matter-of-factness and less and less farcical exaggeration as time went on), definitely had a Beatles theme.

Some snowboarders have backpacks with speakers on them, but the majority who do not often leave it to their brains to provide some tune or other, which brains will do with very little or no conscious prompting whatsoever.

Hey Bungalow Bill, Robin's mind had intoned as she drifted from one side of a snowy run to the other. *What did you kill, Bungalow Bill?* The mantra only grew more dominant when Bill had got too far ahead of or behind her, leaving her to her imagination, ever-vigilant against boredom, that most grave of enemies. *Heeeey Bungalow Bill . . .*

Bill's parents owned a cabin in Tahoe, and the grateful grad student couple had taken advantage of it over a three day weekend. Nothing better than a piney retreat for wintry recreation and maybe just a little debauchery. Sometimes it seemed like life was all about warming cold and stiff limbs by a fire and noticing how cute your boyfriend looked when his cheeks and nose were all pink and bright from the elements. Noticing too, how the pairing of that boyfriend's name and the chorus of the Song of the Day just got funnier the more drinks you had.

But it hadn't been funny when Robin had woken up that morning with the song still playing in her head. More like . . . creepy. *What did you kill?* What kind of a question was that? What *prompted* a question like that?

She smelled eggs and coffee and guessed that 11:30 wasn't too early to get up. Better than 11:15, anyway. Groaning, she rolled out of bed, wrapped herself in a hooded sweatshirt and made a cursory attempt to get the worst of the tangles out of her hair before padding into the kitchen in her PJs.

"How you doin?" Bill had found and was wearing a truly ridiculous apron. Smiling bears frolicked up and down his front. His own hair had suffered abuse from sweat and snow and the tight hug of a beanie over the past couple of days, and was even curlier than usual, spiraling in dark corkscrews.

"Okay," she said. "Coffee."

"Decaf, right?"

"Don't make me hurt you."

He reached across the tiled counter to pour some coffee into a mug. "HAPPY HOLIDAYS!" the mug beamed. It worked, if you counted Valentine's day being a week away or so.

She knew the coffee was too hot to drink and took a sip anyway. Only mildly scalding.

"I was thinking we should clean up pretty soon and get an early-ish start back," Bill said. He shrugged. "Beat the traffic."

"Okay." Robin looked through the living room to the snowy porch outside. Hard to believe just the two of them had made so many footprints on the wooden beams. Seeing the trees helped her nose recognize the thick pine smell they'd been enveloped in for the last couple days. It was thick in a good way, like a warm blanket.

"Am I crazy, or is the smell of pine trees a little like menthol?" she asked.

"Hmm. Maybe you're just associating it with feeling cold."

They ate, gathered up their things, and stuffed them into the car. The boards went up top, in the rack. Then they were rolling, started on their way back to Blackburn, a little rural town in the Monterey Bay area. In the passenger seat, Robin's earworm only seemed to be invigorated as she watched the level of the snow first drop, then fade away entirely as they moved into a warmer climate.

She looked wistfully at the radio/cassette player set below the SUV's digital clock. She'd never wished more that it wasn't broken. They almost always took her car and split the gas when they went places, precisely because then they could listen to music. But her little Corolla could never have made it up these snowy, icy inclines. She wanted something raucous to drive the song out of her head in a hurry. First thing she'd do when she got home was listen to some System of a Down.

She turned to get something of a change of scenery—a new angle at least—and watched the hills and trees rushing by on the other side of Bill's window, his head in the foreground. He had a small little zit next to his ear. A harmless, unassuming thing, not even a whitehead, but she wouldn't mention it because she knew he would be self-conscious. She studied his hands on the wheel, thinking about how he couldn't even be thinking on a conscious level about the tiny adjustments they made to the wheel to keep them on the road.

They were a communicative couple, and after spending a whole weekend together Robin would never have minded the friendly silence in the car if it weren't for that *damn song*.

> *Bill and his elephants were taken by surprise*
> *so Captain Marbles zapped 'im right between the eyyyyes . . .*
> *Hey Bungalow Bill,*
> *What did you kill, Bungalow Bill?*

They pulled over to eat after a couple hours at a brightly-lit fast food place. Murry's seemed to avoid the fast-food vibe by virtue of not being McDonald's or Burger King, and by being adjoined to a produce store. She finally brought it up over their hamburgers.

"You know the song, 'Bungalow Bill?'"

He dabbed ketchup from his lip with his napkin. "'The Continuing Story of Bungalow Bill?' We were singing along with it last night, weren't we?"

She frowned, trying to think of where to begin. "Is it . . . creepy?" When he didn't respond right away she sang the chorus under her breath: "*what did you kill* . . . and so on."

Bill took another bite of his burger and seemed to savor it before tearing himself away. "I can see how it's a little creepy."

"Thank you! I mean, it's so obscure is the thing! 'What did you kill?' Is it some kind of allegory—what the hell is it about?"

"Mmm," Bill said, his mouth full again. He swallowed. "I know that, actually."

"You do?"

"Yeah. It's a story from when John Lennon went to India to see the Maharishi, and stayed with this American family. I guess the mother and son were kind of jerks, because they went out to go tiger hunting." He gave a palms-out, *there you go,* gesture. "So 'he went out tiger hunting with his elephant and gun.'"

Robin clapped her hand to her forehead and laughed. "I always heard it as 'elephuntin' gun'—like some kind of weird play on 'elephant gun."

Bill laughed. "I might like it more your way. Anyway, they go out with some elephants—maybe they were riding the elephants, I'm not sure—and a tiger jumps out at them. The 'Bill' character shoots it, supposedly in self-defense. And the episode made a big enough impression on Lennon for him to write a song about it." He looked away, seemingly distracted by an arguing family two tables over. "But I'm with him—people shouldn't kill tigers."

"No, they shouldn't. Aren't they endangered?'

"I'm not sure. I think so."

"Okay." She made figure eights in her ketchup with a french fry. "The other thing is the Captain Marbles guy. That's really creepy too—the one who "zaps them right between the eyes?"

But Bill was shaking his head. "It's 'Captain Marvel,' the superhero. Lennon's sarcastically referring to Bill—" he pointed at himself—"as this heroic figure for shooting the tiger."

"I've never even heard of Captain Marvel."

"Yeah, he's kind of a lesser-known Superman. He was really popular in the forties, so the Beatles would've known him from their childhood."

"Bill," Robin said, "where would we be without your wealth of useless information?"

"I know, right?" He grinned again. "Captain Marbles doesn't even sound scary—more like a character from a children's show: 'Hey kids, it's Captain Marbles!' 'Yaaay!'"

She laughed. "Are we ready to go?"

"Yeah."

"Let's hit the road. Do you want me to drive?"

"No, I like long drives."

"Cool."

Once again, they were off. India. John Lennon in India.

Robin was pursuing her master's in colonial/postcolonial studies, so the idea triggered a lot pretty easily. Reminded her of that paper that still had a ways to go, for one thing. There'd be time for that soon enough. She let her mind wander. Captain Marvel, not Captain Marbles. Captain Marbles! Ha! Captain Marbles in India. She pictured a British commanding officer, wearing a red coat with little decorative ropes on the shoulders. What kind of man was Captain Marbles? He wouldn't be your everyday career military man, would he?

What did you kill?

No, Captain Marbles was a sadist. She could see him grinning when he caught word of some nationalist rebellion or other, baring tobacco-stained teeth and dark red gums. He'd be grinning at the chance to bash some heads, stop some hearts. If the rebellion was more like a peaceful protest, that wouldn't matter much to him either, would it? She saw the little strips on his chest indicating rank glare back reflected bursts of light as he fired a machine gun into a mass of huddled brown bodies . . . .

She shook her head. What was the matter with her today? She forced herself to watch the world passing by outside their car. As the sun came closer and closer to the horizon, the sky turned a pretty pink—then an almost unbelievable scarlet, and finally a deepening purple.

Robin was almost startled to realize the progress they'd made once it reached this hue. They'd already taken the Monterey exit. And she'd promised to drive part of the way, too! Her seatbelt whirred softly as she leaned to kiss Bill on the cheek. "Nice sunset," she murmured.

"I know," he said. "I was watching it. Hey, look—the streetlights are out here."

So they were. Robin thought they looked odd like that in the dimming twilight, standing up so self-importantly and yet so impotent. Other cars' headlights seemed brighter without the streetlight's glow to give them context.

Soon the city grid-like streets gave way to the rural long and winding road. Robin felt the unique and somehow peculiar sensation that comes when a long car ride suddenly merges into a very familiar drive, when after miles of the new, one feels that she has a passing acquaintance with even that Beetle deserted in a field and the tree with the twisty branches—the *wow, almost home* feeling.

Bill's right hand left the wheel to stroke absently at his cheek. It brushed against the zit Robin had noticed earlier.

"I'm breaking out," he said dolefully.

"It's nothing," Robin said. "I—"

BANG! Her limbs and head flung forward, her feet kicking the end of the seat well as her seatbelt yanked her back. She felt the car pitch forward, then the rear wheels come crashing down to the ground again. The tires shrieked against the pavement. Her face stung, and she didn't know why until she noticed the air bag deflating on her lap.

The car was still now, and she turned to look at Bill look at her in a moment of uncomprehending silence that seemed to stretch on forever. Then Bill peered out through the windshield, where something lay heavily on the road, his headlights shining harshly but unhelpfully on it. There was no traffic.

Wordlessly, Bill turned the key, and the car started again. He drove—slowly, ever so slowly—to the side of the road, and then he quickly turned the engine off again and pushed his door open. Robin scrambled out after him.

"Bill," she breathed, "what did you kil—" and then a wave of panicky queasiness struck her at hearing those words slide out like that. She leaned against the side of the car.

Bill slid back in the driver's seat, one foot still pressed against the dirt outside as he fumbled in the glove box. Stalks of tall grass swayed against Robin's hip, heedless of all. Bill emerged with a flashlight, which shone immediately and faithfully when he pressed the button.

A tiger lay in the road, its jaws crooked open and its eyes glaring blindly. Its body was massive, stretching out across the road to fill half of both lanes, thirteen feet long or more. A dark liquid leaked and puddled around it, and Robin felt her gorge rise when she saw gray ropes and discolored blobs spilling from its belly.

"Are you okay?" Bill was asking her. She realized with a start he had been asking her for some time. His hand was on her shoulder and eyes staring at her in concern.

"Yes," she said.

He had his phone in his hand now, babbling. "A tiger . . . we have to call . . . *forestry service*—" the last phrase uttered with a kind of absurd bewilderment.

Robin snapped back together. "No, Bill, we have to go *right now*." She heard the high shrillness in her voice but couldn't prevent it.

"But—"

She looked at the tiger again, not wanting to take her eyes off of it. It was going to sit up. It would gather its haunches underneath it and spring at them—a killing machine serving its purpose. Its teeth were going to rip open their throats; she saw it happen.

"*We have to go now!*" When was the last time she screamed like that?

Bill listened. Like synchronized swimmers, they ducked back in the car and slammed the doors. They hadn't even checked the damage to the car, but it ran, so they ran with it. The road unspun before them, the dotted line like stitches in a black blanket.

At first Bill seemed hyper-focused on the road, over-tensed after the dramatic reminder of what driving really was: zooming along at a high speed, trusting that there will be nothing in your path. Soon enough, though, he placed his hand on the nape of her neck and softly ran his finger through her hair.

"We're okay, love."

Frustratingly, she felt tears roll down her cheeks. Why had she freaked out back there?

He wiped the tears away with his thumb.

"Oh, keep your eyes on the road," she said, but they both heard a relieved kind of giggle beneath the surface of her words and felt better. She sighed, and opened her mouth to say something about the tiger. "Is it cool if I stay at your place tonight?" was what came out instead.

"Of course."

When they turned onto Bill's road, neither of them noticed that none of the windows in his neighbors' houses had light shining from them. It had become cloudy as well, so that it seemed like the only light in the world came from Bill's headlights, piercing through inky envelopment.

Robin couldn't seem to get her imagination under control. In her mind's eye she saw a pair of shiny black boots walking steadily. Its steps were taken with unhurried casualness, and yet the possessor of those boots seemed to be making a great deal of progress quickly. She saw (no, imagined—how could it possibly be *seeing?*) the boots stop next to a heap of something in the road. The boot nudged it with one shiny toe—there was a sense of something magnificent and noble that had been ruined—and continued on its way, trading steps with its partner.

"Looks like Louis and Kai aren't back yet," Bill said as he parked the car. "Finally here." He slumped back in his seat and closed his eyes. "A *tiger*," he said, as though trying to convince himself. "From a zoo?"

He's tired of driving but you could offer to, Robin's mind whispered quickly. *Just . . . keep going. It's not safe to stop yet.*

"You okay?"

"Um," she said. "Yeah. I'm . . . just in shock a little bit still, I guess."

He put an arm around her and pulled her to him. It was awkward with the stick and parking brake in between them, but it was still nice. It was always nice, Robin realized.

"You saw a tiger, right?" he asked. "Not a mountain lion."

She just nodded. She found that she didn't want to think about it for a little while.

Bill sighed and rubbed her arm. "Should probably check the car," he said. He opened the door and stepped out. Robin could barely see him there in the dark, folding his arms against the cold before he remembered the flashlight still in his sweater pocket and shone it at the car.

She looked at her door handle, and decided to pull it.

She got out and joined Bill. A part of her had been wondering if there would be no damage done to the car at all, if the whole mad thing had been some kind of hallucination.

But the surface of the hood snarled and rippled out from the point of impact. The headlights had been spared and the car was tall enough to protect the windshield, but anyone who glanced at the vehicle would know right away that something had forcefully disagreed with it. Robin sighed.

"I'm sorry, Bill."

"Yeah . . ." he said heavily. Robin sensed he was thinking of the animal they had left in the middle of the road, a trap for some other driver.

"And I've never even hit a squirrel," he said. "Well, let's just go in."

They went to the door of his house and he fumbled the key into the lock. Stepping in, Bill performed that most automatic of actions: he flicked the light switch. Robin heard it. But nothing happened.

"Power's out," he said. "Oh—that explains the streetlights. Hang on, I've got candles somewhere." First he went to the phone. Robin watched him pick it up and listen before setting it back in its cradle. "The phone's out, too," he said. "Think somebody hit a telephone pole?"

Cell phone coverage was spotty to nonexistent this far from the city, which meant that call to the forestry service would not be made by them.

Settled on the couch in candlelight, Robin began to feel more and more uncomfortable, not relaxed. She saw a figure turn down Bill's road with a snappish right face, never deviating from its speed. With her regular vision she watched shadows cast by flickering candlelight jerk about on Bill's wall like puppets on violent marionette strings. Her mouth soured at even a sip of the beer Bill had gotten from the fridge.

They sat wordlessly on the couch after that as if, Robin thought, they were waiting for something. She didn't even want to sit, not after hours in the car, but felt unable to get up. She could have paced, but felt paralyzed.

She found herself thinking of the last painting she'd made—way back when she was an undergrad and had time for that. She was in the shower when she saw a sparrow flying high up, way high up with a forest stretching out far below it. The picture in her head had the viewer looking down at the bird, too, from just a little bit above it, poised thousands of feet in the air. As soon as she got out she'd toweled off and gotten straight to work on it. The image seemed to come effortlessly, down to the oily rainbow sheen on the black parts of the sparrow's coloring. She hadn't thought up that painting. The painting had come to her. She'd just tried to copy it down right.

She thought of going to that museum exhibit with her friend and looking at the paintings by that German guy—Goethe? No, he was a writer. Friedrich, that was it. Caspar David Friedrich and his stark, leafless trees in the snow. "Ugh," Naomi had said. "How depressing."

"No it's not," she'd replied. "It's beautiful—peaceful, even."

Boots crunched past the houses of Bill's neighbors.

"Bill," she said at last, in a high voice she didn't recognize.

"Yes? What is it?"

He knows something's wrong, she thought, her head against his shoulder, *but only because he knows* I'm *uneasy*.

"Do you think," she asked in a dreamy, hesitating voice, "artists . . . songwriters, whatever . . . *channel* something when they . . . create?"

Bill frowned, his way of asking for more detail.

She continued, speaking the words as they surfaced in her mind. "I mean, the creative process is . . ." (*mysterious, unknowable*) "weird."

He just listened.

"And do you think that an artist could channel something—by accident—bad? Something from somewhere else?"

Crunch, crunch. Black boots. Black shiny boots. Crisp, merciless uniform.

"And then do you think . . . since, um, a big part of . . . *art* . . . depends on the . . . audience—" *crunch, crunch* "someone could . . . see or . . . *hear* a work of art a certain way and . . . let something in? If the artist created some kind of door—with a song—and then something needed someone to hear that song just the right way for the door to be opened?"

"I don't know," Bill said, and his voice proved his words.

"I think I do," she whispered.

She was kissing him when the door flew open. She caught a glimpse of a tall figure, of gleaming strips on a chest and of a grin made out of cruelty.

*   *   *

When they came and looked at the couple after Bill's roommate Kai found them, nothing looked wrong with them. The coroner couldn't find anything wrong at all—no reason that their hearts should have stopped beating and their lungs should have stopped squeezing in and out. The only thing unusual at all was that both of them had a burn-like mark at the top of the bridge of their noses—a little black dot no larger than the pimple next to Bill Hubbard's ear.

THE COP

I got a sinking feeling in my stomach when I saw the flashing lights in my rearview mirror. I was driving along a long boring stretch of highway all by myself. Rocking out a little bit to the Chili Peppers, if you want to know the truth. I hadn't seen another car in an hour. I didn't know why more people didn't take the uncrowded highway, but I was glad they didn't. Nothing can spoil a drive like traffic. Some big, slow truck you could get stuck behind or that oh so thrilling neck and neck race between two semis hogging both lanes. Maybe the extra half hour before the Madera exit was too much for most drivers, but I think CA 991 just seems to be out of reach of people's radar. God knows I found it by accident.

Science knows I found it by accident, as I and my atheist friends say when we catch ourselves saying something religious-sounding just because it's part of how everyone talks. *Oh my Scientific Method.* What the fuck, my mom still says "By Jove," and it's not as though she's an ancient Roman.

Anyway I caught a blur of movement that proved to be a chip car roaring out from behind one of the only starving trees around, dying in the dry heat. It started wailing on its siren, and there were those flashing lights, too, in case I didn't see what he was getting at. I glanced at my speedometer. I'd never heard of anyone getting pulled over for going 70 in a 65 zone.

I put on the brakes and pulled onto the dirt shoulder. I should have slowed more first, because I threw up so much dust the patrol car became only a vague dark shape in the clouds behind me. "God damn it." Good luck trying to un-God that one. Copernicus doesn't damn, just like nobody ever said Isaac Newton died for your sins.

When the dust cleared, I watched the cop's door open and a tall, built man step out. He crunched his way over the grit to me, and I got a better look at him standing beside my open window. The man wasn't fat, but there was clearly a fat man lurking inside him, biding his time until he retired from the force. His dark blue shirt bulged only modestly, and his pinkly overshaved cheeks were just round enough to give you that impression. But he'd been doing his best to contain his would-be fat in muscle, and there was a lot of that, too. OFFICER JENNINGS, the strip on his breast pocket read. He took off his cop sunglasses and looked at me unsmilingly.

"License and registration."

I had them ready, handed them to him. It was starting to get hot in my car. My car's air conditioning has never worked, and without the wind blowing through my windows I could already feel the sweat gathering against the back of my shirt. Nobody stays in parked cars in the Central Valley in July.

Then Officer Jennings did his first unsettling thing. He peered at my driver's license, his eyes flicking across it, and then bent the ends toward each other until it snapped neatly in two. *Crack.* Then he quickly ripped my registration paper in half, put the two halves against each other, and ripped them again. He dropped my license and the ripped paper on the dirt and stepped on them, grinding them in with his boot.

This whole time Jennings' face remained clear and emotionless. He looked up at me again.

"Get out of the vehicle, Brandon," he said.

I didn't move.

The cop shot his arm through my window and grabbed my chest-length hair.

"Hey!" I yelled, and then there was an overriding pain in my scalp as my shoulder was bashed against the side of my door. Something popped in my neck and I realized I was simply going to be pulled through my window head first. I fumbled at my door handle and swung the door open. I would have sprawled onto the ground, but instead the pressure on my scalp only increased and I literally swung from his fist. My nerves screamed and the skin from my forehead to my eyes was trying to untether from my skull. Scrabbling my legs beneath me, I found purchase and managed to stand up.

"I want to show you something," Jennings said.

"Let go of me," I said as firmly as I could. I was still having trouble believing any of this was happening.

"Come over here." He began to walk around my car, still holding most of hair in his clenched fist.

"Let the fuck go!" I yelled. He kept dragging me, so I grabbed his wrist with one hand and grasped at his fingers with the other. I pulled hard at his ring finger and the rest fell away, releasing me.

Then he belted me in the face. Heat spread from my nose to the rest of my face, and the bright world around me went a little gray. Jennings grabbed me by the front of my shirt and hauled me to the back of my car.

"What is that?" he demanded.

It was the lone sticker on my bumper. U.S. **OUT** OF IRAQ, it stated flatly.

"A bumper sticker," I said.

This time I dodged his fist coming at my face. But not the next swing. It caught me hard in the stomach, and all the breath went out of me in one push. I keeled over, but didn't fall.

"No," Jennings said. "It's the mark of a traitor. We don't need you in Fresno County." He advanced toward me again.

As if to make up for my brain's initial, fatal slowness, I realized two things very quickly. I realized this man was going to keep hurting me, and was going to hurt me badly. And I realized that my best, terrifying course of action was nonviolent resistance, deep South 1960s style. There were no witnesses to this police brutality, but I was going to put this man behind bars. I had to hold onto that future to face the present. And when I faced down Officer Jennings in court, there wouldn't be a single bruise on his body to support any claim of self-defense on his part.

Unless he planned to kill me.

This time his fist caught me in the mouth, splitting my lower lip open.

"You fucking traitors can't be tolerated," he said. "You'll destroy this country from the inside out."

He threw another punch. I dodged it but he was too fast. He grabbed me by my shoulders and slammed me against the side of the car.

"Faggot," he snarled. "Men cut their hair. Men take the time to shave. Because men—American men—have a sense of character. Your fucking beard you're trying to turn *Arab*, be a complete commie terrorist *faggot*."

"I won't fight you," I said, trying hard to keep my voice level. My voice sawed in my throat. "I know my rights, and if you know what's best for your own interests you'll stop with what you've done already, because I'm going to report this."

He drove an elbow hard into my ribs and I fell to the ground, where I put my arms over my head and curled up into the fetal position. I pulled my knees up against my stomach protectively.

Jennings jacked a boot hard into my tailbone, setting off an explosion of pain. Then I felt his baton for the first time, slamming down on my ribs. More baton blows hammered my arms and fingers where I held them against my skull. I screamed and willed for a car. With all my might I willed someone to drive by.

He pummeled me with his steel-toed boots, giving a series of fast kicks, one after the other after the other, and then alternating to really wind up for the blow. He picked me off the ground and drove me head first into the dirt, the pavement, the car, his boot. I tried to protect my crotch, dropping an arm from my head to brace between my legs, my wrist intersecting with his kicks. He mashed my balls hard, but didn't destroy them. He kicked me in the face, overcoming my desperate attempts to dodge or block the blows. No cars came. He grabbed me by the hair again and slammed my face into the road. I felt the tip of my nose scrape off against the pavement like an eraser.

I'd lost all track of time when he propped me up against my car one last time. I looked at him through a haze. Every part of my body was ringing. I saw the world the world through the slit of my left eye—the right had swollen shut. My lips puffed against spaces once filled by teeth.

Jennings pulled his pistol out.

"I'm going to kill you faggot. And then I'm going to look up your family. I'm going to shoot them in their throats. I'm going to look up who you're fucking. Your boyfriend, huh faggot? I'm going to put this gun up his ass the way he likes it. Blow his gut out from the inside. Your girlfriend? My knife up her cunt."

He cocked the gun. So, he was going to kill me then. That changed things. And I thought he'd follow through on his threat to my family. The man reeked of determination. He'd rape and murder Jenna—and my ex-boyfriend, too, if the bigot could handle complexity in sexuality.

I had a hunch he could. My life depended on it.

He brought the gun up against my forehead.

"Wait," I said. I pressed my hand below his belly. What was there was hard as metal. I suspected he sprung it shortly after his first blow.

"I know what you really want," I said. It came out in a croak, and I was suddenly aware of blood running down from my scalp.

Jennings said nothing. The moment spun out. And then he grinded against my open palm.

"That's right," I said, and slid my hand down his jeans. I let my fingers drop down to his balls. "I'll take care of you. No one needs to get shot."

The gun dropped away from my head. Jennings stared into my face, I thought I'd never seen anything as ugly as his eyes straining from their sockets.

I grabbed his balls and squeezed as hard as I could.

Jennings roared, his face strawberry red. I pulled my hand out and grabbed the gun from his hand, his grip completely gone.

His eyes, already wet with pain, widened just before I swung the pistol in a wide sidewise arc to crack next to his eye. Jennings hit the ground. I stood over him with the gun in my hand and suddenly felt something like adrenaline surging throughout my entire body, wiping out even the pain. It was hate I felt. I felt hate and rage and suddenly, power. All the power in the world. I leveled the gun at his head.

"Don't kill me!" he shouted. "Please! I'm sorry!"

I shot him in the shin. Seeing the bone shatter and the blood spurt made me feel very good. His scream of agony made me feel even better. I would have liked to jam the now hot tip of the pistol down his throat then, but I was taking no chances of him grabbing the gun from me. I scanned the horizon. No cars still. Good, then.

"You're going to say something for me," I said. "And mean it, or I'll kill you. Do you understand?"

Jennings nodded.

"Say that you are what's wrong with the world. Tell me you know it's people like you who fill this world with hate and murder and pain."

Jennings just looked at me. I shot him in the knee.

"Aaagh!"

"That was your last warning," I told him.

"*Jeezus*," Jennings said in a long shuddering inhale.

"*Say it!*" I screamed, and felt myself jerk towards the edge. I gritted my teeth to get a hold of myself. Then spat one out. A gristled red and white thing.

"I am what's bad in the world. People like me make it filled with hate and killing and hurt."

"That's right," I said softly.

I threw the gun away. It didn't go very far. I wasn't in any shape to throw anything. But I wasn't worried about Jennings retrieving it without kneecaps. I called an ambulance, and we waited together under the hot bright sun.

DREAMBOATS

He was lifted easily and helplessly into the air, his legs held by one massive paw, his torso by another. The teeth punctured his middle, tore into him.

Zach came to, panting. His eyes were wide and wild as he took in his surroundings: a dingy room, partly illuminated by a single harsh desk lamp. Eric smiled at him wanly.

"What a rush," Zach said.

"Of course, man," said Eric.

Zach put his arms behind his head and sank onto his back on the floor. He could feel his heart pounding away in his chest like someone was playing sixteenth notes on a drum. He could swear it was beating hard enough to wear out his shirt.

"Hooo!" he said. He let himself just take in Eric's basement without talking. Without trying to think too much about anything. He let his eyes trace the unpainted wooden boards, following the lines and dark circles that once ran around inside a tree. He thought he saw a spider, but it was too dark to tell. There were a couple easy chairs; Eric was sitting in one, but Zach wasn't surprised to find himself on the floor. He forced himself to slow his breathing.

"Is my water still around?" he asked.

Eric tossed him a bottle still half full. He drained it. Eric didn't say anything. He was too good a dealer for that. He knew when to just let his patrons recover. When talking would be a nuisance for them.

"Where you goin?" Zach's roommate had asked when he left their apartment for the smog outside and the yellow horizon.

"Coffee shop. To do some reading."

"Yeah I believe that," Emilio said, holding his place in his magazine. "If you see Eric, be cool. That guy acts all mellow, but I've heard a lot of things."

"Okay." Zach had lived with Emilio long enough to give his advice the casual disrespect of a sibling.

"I mean it. Hey, keep this in mind—he's a shitty businessman. He cares more about his own petty influence and reputation than money. He's not all there."

"Alright."

"Is Remi still hanging around him?'

Zach closed the door around his reply and tried to hide his smirk. "You must already know. You know everything else."

"You should pay him!" Emilio yelled, and then Zach did grin. When you yelled through a closed door, you lost the argument even if you did get in the last word.

Now he was in the belly of the beast, or so Emilio would have it. But it was only a basement. Aluminum barrels lined the walls. To the unfamiliar eye, they would have looked like canisters of helium or $Co2$. Tubes were attached to the top of each, with wires tipped with sticky circles that reminded Zach of the reinforcers he used back in middle school to keep his papers in his notebook. Dreamboats was the slang Zach liked most for them. A full sensory hallucinatory experience, better than any drug, in his humble opinion.

That monster one. That was a kick. *Hoo*, was it. When you're on the dreamboat, you don't remember that you're really just sitting in a room with neuron stimulators stuck to your scalp. You think it's real. Your memories comply with the hallucination too.

"Can I have that meadow one now?" Zach said.

"Yeah, sure." Eric went to all the canisters and glanced over them. He pulled one out and pushed a small button on its side, causing a tiny disc to slide out. Eric held the disc between his thumb and forefinger, looked it over, and nodded.

"Top notch, man," he said, and pulled the canister over to Zach. It made a hollow reverberating sound as it slid over the floor. Zach took the wires on top of the tube and pulled them out, untangling a few that had spun around each other. He stuck them one at a time to his scalp, to the base of his skull, and behind his ears, where his mother still told him to wash carefully when she called.

He looked out at a green meadow, his skin warm from the sun. He was sitting in some grass near a clear and shallow river that tinkled around rocks like a wind chime as it flowed by. The clouds were puffy above the mountains in the distance.

Whirrrrr. He turned sharply to see a hummingbird zip closely behind him, then pull to a midair stop and hesitate before blurring off again. It had been close enough for Zach to see the gleam off the red feathers on its chest.

The tall grass had been dotted with color: patches of wildflowers everywhere. With a sigh he let himself fall onto his back, his hands cupped behind his head. The grass cushioned him and brushed gently against his cheek.

Then he heard the swishing sound of someone running through grass. He sat up to see a girl with light hair streaming behind her as she ran towards him. Her smile rivaled the sun.

"Zach!" she called, right before she reached him and threw herself on him.

"Oof!" he said, and then they were laughing as she rolled over him to lay in the grass, her head touching his as they looked into the sky.

"It's too beautiful a day to spend alone," she said.

"You're right," Zach said. He kissed her. Her fingers combed through his hair.

Dusty beams suddenly shot out over the sky. Zach thumped his head against the floor, his arms jerking in, no longer holding anyone.

"Back so soon?" Eric asked. He had just started a joint.

"I was gypped!" Zach said. "That was over right away!"

Eric shrugged. "It's your head, man. Lots of people can't handle two trips in a row. Don't blame the dreamboats."

Zach stared at the walls, which seemed three times grimier than before. It seemed the grease of ages had sunk into these walls. He felt the still air and artificial light crowding in on him, sticking to him. He wanted to shower—no, he wanted to go back to the river and swim in it.

He wanted her. The loneliness crippled him, bent him on the floor so he couldn't move. He couldn't handle that part of the trip, having something so dear so briefly only to be snatched back again as suddenly as though a bucket of ice water had been poured on him. He felt that loneliness at the base of everything, a darkness that pushed its tentacles into every nook and cranny of his inner life. Into his hopes, his ambitions, his efforts to be happy.

"I want the monster one again," he said.

Eric raised his eyebrows. "No problem," he said. "Except . . . when are you going to pay me back for all your trips over these past weeks, man?"

"When you stop fucking my sister," Zach snapped.

Eric stared at him. "Remi and I are really happy together."

Zach said nothing. The idea of his sister stuck with this lowlife began to feel physically repulsive to him.

"Give me the boat."

"Seriously, man, when are you going—"

"I get paid Friday!" he shouted. "Fuck you! Have I ever not paid you once I had the money? All I can say is you better be wearing condoms, asshole. Give me the boat—that's your job, isn't it?"

Something flashed in Eric's eyes that Zach didn't like. For a moment he was sure the man was going to belt him one. But Eric only slid him the canister wordlessly.

In the blackness, he inhaled a rich smell of dust and dead grass. He opened his eyes to find himself on a moonlit dirt road, surrounded by tall brown vegetation. He knew it to be brown though it appeared silvery under the light of the full moon. This world was all silver and black—silver trees and silver roads cut by black shadows and silhouettes.

Something's different this time, Zach thought, and that thought was followed by: *"this time?"*

He walked slowly down the road, contented just to amble. He hummed a tune from a song he'd heard on the radio that day. He didn't know the words. The moon was a pale face, so bright he could easily read by it. He felt a deep calm, here in the night air.

Then he heard a sound. He turned and saw a shape far down the road. Or thought he saw one. He squinted. Was it a man, a fellow traveler? He'd let him travel in peace. He never was one to particularly enjoy the company of a stranger when he could be alone with his thoughts—when he could hum to himself and no one was around to hear. He walked on.

The outline of a large foothill rose out of the darkness. He kept his eye on that. The friend's house where he'd be staying was at the base of Corlew Mountain, and he'd probably be getting worried at Zach's lateness.

He heard a canine snort.

Zach turned to look behind him again. There was a figure there now, just passing under the shadow of a large oak. Something was funny about it, though. Was he some sort of hunchback, the way he walked? The only thing Zach could put his finger on was that something was wrong with the traveler's dimensions.

It came out of the shadows, and Zach saw it for what it was. It was something from a nightmare, the creature he'd known as a small child lurked in the hallway just outside his room, the reason he'd slept with a nightlight.

It was a wolf, walking erect, twice the size of a man. The moonlight shone clearly down its furrowed face, its eyebrows knotted in a cruel expression around dark eyes, its fangs hooking past its snout.

Zach edged his way toward the underbrush. And then the beast ran for him. Zach watched its legs pump, its paws gripping the dirt, and then his paralysis broke and he ran too, into the fields. He ran down the side of a dried creek and scrambled up the other, but he never had any chance. He could hear something huge moving through the brush with a speed and efficiency he could never hope to match. The moon swung crazily in his stumbling flight. And then it was upon him.

An arm clenched around his shoulder and wrenched him around, claws digging gashes in his flesh. He saw the thing, its eyes blazing as it reared back and thought in an instant of Eric's eyes just before he sent him off. In that second, Zach remembered everything, and perfect comprehension dawned on him. It had been murder in Eric's eyes.

The monster brought his jaws down and Zach, a slave to his instincts to the bitter, useless end, raised his forearms to block his neck. The beast's teeth crunched through them. It twisted its neck and ripped his right arm from his body

He was filled with unimaginable pain. This was real, there was no doubt this was real. If ignorance is bliss, Zach spent his last seconds of life in intellectual as well as physical agony. He died every time, he realized. Every time, this thing kills me.

This is the last time.

THE MISSING FORT

He killed himself a month after Sheila broke up with him. After spring break he drove most of the way back to Santa Cruz, where they went to college, then unbuckled his seatbelt and hurdled over the top of Hecker Pass. It was a terribly effective suicide. He bounced around the inside of his little Corolla like a grasshopper in a tin can, then shot through the windshield, where he stuck half in, half out as the car rolled over him before it finally lodged up against a tree halfway down the mountain.

Sheila wished he'd chosen a different way to do it. The car crash seemed so terrifying to her, and she didn't like thinking of his last moment alive spent that way. She wished he'd left a note, but was afraid of what it might have said. You bitch, it might have said. You made me do this.

She watched the RIPs and tributes pile up on his Facebook page. Several people wrote about memories—*remember on tour when we rocked the jazz band*—*I remember when you were there for me when my parents divorced*—*I used to look up to you*—each heartbreaking in its own way. She hadn't known what to say in such a public forum, and in the end she kept it brief.

Goodbye, James. She tried to write an apology but it never came out right. It's not your fault, everyone told her. But James would be alive if she hadn't left him. *Goodbye James*, she wrote. *I love you.* It wasn't love in the way he'd wanted it in the end, in the way it once was, but yes, she loved him.

It had been so good in the beginning. Sheila was fresh out of high school, and when she fell for James she realized she'd never really been in love before. She thought she'd love him forever, and told him so, something he reminded her of bitterly when she found she'd changed her mind. But things were so good. He was caring, he was beautiful, and damned if he wasn't one *smart* motherfucker. When he got on his soapbox and talked politics, it wasn't hard to see herself as the first lady twenty years in the future. She gave her virginity to him, and it hurt, yes, but not as badly as she'd feared, and the pain gave way quickly to a pleasure deeper than anything he'd created with his fingers and tongue. It was the whole *everything* of it, inhaling the smell of his hair and the dust and the grass outside, far from the city with the full moon and the stars shining down on them.

When the fighting started it was like the world's most stubborn unwanted guest, settling down deep in an easy chair in the middle of their relationship. Over time he'd become less diplomatic in their increasingly fraught arguments, calling her things like high-maintenance and clingy. Would it kill her to give him a Saturday with just his friends? No, but the friend he wanted to see the most was his smelly little glass pipe and the never-ending supply of sticky green herb to put in it. Not that she hadn't tried it, and it could be fun, but more often it made her anxious, and it made him stupid and distant from her.

She decided to go to his funeral, in spite of everything. She wore a black dress that she couldn't see herself ever wearing again and sat with his friends. To her relief, they greeted her warmly—she'd been so afraid they'd hate her. She hadn't expected the open casket, which struck her as almost unbearably bleak.

She saw James' father, bent over in his chair, his posture identical to James' when she'd told him she was leaving. His hands cradled his head, hiding his face. His sister and mother rested their heads on each other's shoulders. The two of them made an island in a sea of grief, and at the thought she lost her composure. It was only that that was such a *James* thought; he had been the poetic one—the only boy who'd ever written her love poems. *My fort*, he'd called her in one.

> *I'll build a fort with you*
> *As long as you keep being my fort.*

But she couldn't do that for him. She'd stopped being his fort. She cried onto his housemate's shoulder. It was flat and feminine and not James'.

The pastor was wrapping up his eulogy, and there were indignant rumbles from James' friends at how religious it was. James had been an outspoken atheist—the kind of thing that got smoothed over when you died young and belonged to a religious family. She couldn't bring herself to care much about it.

She found herself in line to file past his casket. She didn't know how she could face him. Further up, his mother bent over her son's body. From where she stood, the body looked just like him, not . . . (*mangled*) . . . messed up. His mother, a small, pretty woman, faltered, then straightened and turned. Sheila looked directly into her face.

It was unrecognizable. It twisted in pain as a silent river coursed from each eye. Then she saw Sheila and her face perverted itself even more. Her nostrils flared in a snarl and her lips pulled flat to show her teeth. There was no trace of the woman who never failed to hug her and compliment her on her outfit. She raised a shaking hand.

"You *killed* him!" she shrieked, stumbling forward. "*He wasn't good enough for you?*" Her voice raised to a hellish pitch: she was screaming through her sobs. "You *murderer!* You *murdered* my son!"

"Alice!" James' stepfather caught her and pulled her to him. She emitted a keening noise, and collapsed against him.

Sheila fled.

Alice mailed her an apology a few days later; even when Sheila ran to her car there were James' friends and relatives grabbing her arm, assuring her that they didn't blame her. But the guilt was a pit deep in her stomach, sending shoots all through her body. She wasn't a murderer, no, but had she committed something like romantic manslaughter? She thought of them happy, downtown in Santa Cruz, happy at the lake, happy in his bed.

Their last weekend together they had had a huge fight, one that they couldn't seem to end. He'd wanted to retreat to the living room to calm down, to smoke a bowl, and she did what she had never done before, taking the little bag in which he kept his weed and pipe and holding it beneath her breasts in her folded arms.

"If it's not something you *need*, it shouldn't be a big deal," she said.

"I don't need it, I'm just fucking pissed off at you and want to relax." He held out his palm. She didn't budge.

"Christ," he said, the eyes that had so often looked straight into hers with tenderness now filled with anger. "You already got your way on *everything* tonight. I'm here, with you, instead of with my friends in town for the weekend—who I never get to see—even though I'm going to spend the entire weekend at your house."

He had to make it sound like such a chore.

"Just give me my shit."

"No. Don't smoke tonight."

"Who do you think you are?" he exploded. "What makes you think you can control me?" He balled his hands into fists and struck the doorway, stamping his foot. At the gesture so childish, a thought flashed through her mind as clearly as though it was printed there: It's over. You have to leave.

But she didn't for another week.

He came to see her a couple weeks after the break-up. He told her how desperately he loved her. That he had thrown away his pipe and weed, would never take another toke. "Do you miss me?" he asked.

"As a friend."

"Don't you love me anymore?"

She searched her heart. The love she'd had for him, once so strong it filled her whole body, permeated every thought and action, had all been boiled away.

Sheila got another letter after she'd gone back to school and was trying to concentrate on essays and homework, obligations that seemed more trivial than ever now. She got a nasty shock when she opened the letter and pulled out another envelope with James' familiar messy cursive on the front: *Sheila.* Next to it was a note from his sister explaining that James' suicide notes—several of them, addressed to different people, had been knocked behind his desk and only now found. James Mennen, disorganized even in death.

With trembling fingers she tore open the letter.

Dear Sheila,

I'm so sorry for the pain I've caused you by taking my life. I hate to think of you having feelings of guilt, and I didn't do this because you left. On the contrary, you were an amazingly bright time in my usually unhappy life. I'm so grateful for the love you found for me. It's not your fault things didn't work out; we were almost but not quite right for each other. We just have different styles of loving. And I'm just not cut out for this world. Thank you, for everything.

Love,
James

That night Sheila rose out of sleep to see James standing just inside her doorway. Instinctively, she resisted waking fully, knowing that would banish him forever. He came to her bed and she cupped his face with her hands. His cheeks and jaw were real to her touch. She ran her fingers through his hair, looked into his eyes and kissed his lips. As always, they were soft and firm in all the right ways. Wordlessly, she pulled back her sheets and he slid in next to her. She cradled his head to her chest and fell asleep with his arms around her and his breath warm against her skin.

BEARS ON THE ROAD TO DAMASCUS

"Please make yourself comfortable. The police are on your side."

"Officer, this has been the most overwhelming experience of my life. I think . . . I'm in shock, a little bit—"

"I have no doubt that you are."

"—and if there's any way this can wait until tomorrow? I'd just love to go home."

"I'm sorry, Paul, but it's our policy to get accounts as soon as possible whenever there's a death involved, when everything is fresh in people's heads. Can I offer you some coffee?"

"I'd prefer gin, to be honest."

"Can you settle for whiskey?"

"That'd be just fine."

I sent for the whiskey and asked for a glass for myself. Some people don't mind being the only one drinking, but I wanted to make sure Paul Conway was comfortable. And God, I'd wanted a drink the first time I'd killed a man.

Paul drank his whiskey with an expression of deep relief, his face as smooth and steady as if his glass was filled with water. He sighed, then leaned forward.

"Detective Winthrop, it happened like this."

> We were walking home from a late showing of Avatar, that new movie with the blue aliens. I've never been mugged before in my whole life, but as soon as I saw this guy, I just got a certain feeling that it was going to happen. He looked like your average homeless guy, maybe a little more ragged than usual, standing a block away from the metro station, near the Salvation Army. I think it was the

way he was looking at us straight on, right at my face. It wasn't the—I don't know, almost apologetic look people usually have when they ask for money. That feeling almost made me cross the street so we wouldn't walk past him, but I didn't do it. I don't know, I would've felt too embarrassed to do that. I had that feeling, yes, but I guess I thought I was too rational to act on things like that. I'm not superstitious, or religious—

"It's okay, Paul," I broke in. "You don't need to explain yourself about that. What happened when you got to the homeless man?" The homeless man whose name we didn't know yet.

Well, he stood right in the middle of the sidewalk, blocking us, you know. Then he pulled out the pistol, which was small and black and . . . utilitarian, I guess. Not something that would look very mean in a movie, but it was a gun, so it was plenty scary.
"Gimme your money," he said. "Hurry."
I gave Isabelle a quick look just as she gave me one, and we read in each other's eyes that, yeah, of course we were going to give him our money. It wasn't worth getting killed over. I started to pull out my credit cards as she was reaching in her purse.
"Gimme your whole fucking wallet," he said. His voice was low, quietly menacing. I gave him my whole fucking wallet.
So did Isabel, and when he grabbed the wallet from her, still pointing the pistol at me, I saw him look at her in a way I didn't like at all. A couple seconds passed before he said anything, and they dragged on like an eternity. When you're a kid, you think the last five minutes before summer vacation take forever, but try waiting at gunpoint. I became more and more sure he was going to shoot us, and was trying to think of how to attack him first.
Then: "You're coming with me," he said to my girlfriend, moving the point of the gun onto her. If I lunged at him, would he shoot her first? He stared hungrily at her breasts.
I thought I could reason with him. "No. Hold on," I said. "Don't do this. You just got enough money from us to buy consensual sex from a hooker. But if you try to rape her, you'll be caught, and you'll end up serving a life sentence. More likely, you'll get the death

sentence. You'll end up in the chair. They'll kill you. It's not worth it. Buy a hooker."

I know people usually don't get the death sentence for rape, and I know we don't use the electric chair anymore. Whatever. I was counting on him not knowing it. He also didn't know I was a bleeding-heart who'd opposed capital punishment my whole life. Whatever. Whatever. Whatever.

"More whiskey, Paul?" I asked. The man was becoming agitated, and I thought if he said *whatever* one more time he'd break down. He nodded, and I poured him a generous glass from the Jameson bottle on the table.

There wasn't anybody on the street but us. "Shut up," the man said. From what I could tell, he wasn't affected by what I'd said at all. I put my arm around Isabel's shoulder and pulled her to me. "You'll be caught," I said again. "You'll be jailed, and probably killed. Do yourself a favor and just go find a whore. There are other ways to get laid."

Isabelle wasn't saying anything, but she was trembling against me. I thought I knew her well enough to guess what she was thinking: that she'd rather be raped than have either of us killed. I'd rather she be raped than have her killed, but I wasn't going to give her up without a fight.

The man looked at me with jaundiced eyes and smiled. "But why should I go looking for it when I've got such great pussy right here?" He reached out the arm not holding the gun and squeezed Isabel's breast.

I grabbed his other arm and shoved it away, the gun pointing way out to his side. I punched him in the face as hard as I could and blood gushed instantly from his nose. Isabelle yelled and kicked at his groin but the man dodged it and her foot connected with his thigh instead. There was an enormous explosion; the gun had gone off and it was deafening. Then he swung it back towards me. I grabbed his wrist and pushed the gun up above his head. With my other hand I found his fingers wrapped around the gun and yanked at his pinkie. I heard it snap just before he roared with pain. I pulled the gun away. He was moving fast to hit me.

"Shoot him, Paul, shoot him!" Isabelle shrieked and I pushed the gun right against his forehead and pulled the trigger. There was that deafening bang again, the loudest thing I've ever heard, gunshots on TV are a joke, and he fell down with blood pouring from the hole in his head. There was so much of it.

Then we called you.

I reached over the table to touch Paul's shoulder. "You acted in complete self-defense," I told him. Now that he'd finished telling the story he looked tired and pukey and forty instead of twenty-five. "Thank you for your excellent, detailed account. Robert will give you a ride home now, to be with Isabel. If there's anything at all you need, please give me a call." I slid him my card. "You've been through a very traumatic experience." As if he needed me to tell him that.

"I just . . . never thought I'd kill anybody," he said.

"Me neither," I told him, wanting him to get I knew how he felt. "With me it was some convenience store robbery nut job with a gun. Even when I became a cop, I didn't think I'd ever kill anyone either. But Paul, you did the right thing."

He nodded, and left.

I thought that was the end of the whole sordid affair. It would have been, if anything very interesting had happened on the central coast that day. But it was a slow news day, and that's why the Santa Roma *Seal* ran the story of an attempted rape and a self-defense homicide. Probably a few hundred thousand people read about Paul Conway and his adventure with a man of the streets. Some of them wrote letters to the editor, to the effect that we all ought to finally crack down on The Homeless Problem. Another said it was time to crack down on The Handgun Problem. Nobody suggested cracking down on The Rape Problem, probably because rape's been around longer than handguns and cities for people to be homeless in. And one of those people who read the article came to see me at my office.

"My name is Jackson Comeau," the man said, extending a worn but clean hand. His jacket was stained, but his hair and face were also clean. I appreciated the trouble he'd gone to. It can be hard to keep the grime off when you're a member of The Homeless Problem.

"I know the man the newspaper said tried to rape that girl," he said. "His name's Bob Espinoza—everyone calls him Bear. I know he couldn't have done this."

I eyed him from behind my desk. I wasn't exactly eager to get to the mountain of paperwork waiting for me, but I had just enough of a work ethic to care that the chief would be pissed if I didn't have it done by the end of the day.

"Then he didn't," I said. "How do you know the man we're talking about is your friend Bear?" I gave him my most skeptical eyebrow raise to distract him from my hand, which was scribbling *Bob Espinoza* right under *Jackson Comeau.*

Jackson handed me a folded newspaper. Underlined with a blunt pencil was the line that tipped him off.

"An unidentified homeless man whose distinguishing features include a sunburst tattoo on his bicep," he recited. "I was there when he inked the tattoo on himself."

I sipped my coffee.

"I came to you because I knew you could be sympathetic," the bum said. "I knew you know what it's like."

And there it was. I noted Jackson hadn't said *please* this whole time and warmed to him. He hadn't come to kiss my ass and beg me to listen to him. It was hard to hold onto any dignity for the Jackson Comeaus of the world—and once upon a time, for the Winthrops.

"So you read the paper pretty often, Jackson?" I asked, pouring him a cup of coffee.

"Why not?" He grinned. "They're my streets being covered."

Jackson knew about me because I am, in my own small way, something of a celebrity. I got my own feature in the *Seal*, a feel-good piece to balance all the not-so good news coming out of the middle east. "**HOMELESS TO HERO:** FORMER HOMELESS MAN RISES TO RANK OF DETECTIVE AND SOLVES GONZALES MURDER CASE," the headline read, if I remember correctly. And I do.

My secretary tapped on the glass window of my door. Miss Hong was a smart little thing who rejected every advance I ever made. You see how smart she is.

"I just wanted to let you know they got the dentals back and identified the assailant."

I eyed Jackson and raised my palms, summoning the name.

"His name was Robert Richard Espinoza," Charlotte Hong said.

"Any word on the gun?"

"Unlicensed."

"All right, Mr. Comeau," I said. "I believe I'd better listen to your story."

He sipped his coffee.

"Thank you, Miss Hong," I called after my beautifully unobtainable secretary.

Jackson stroked his cheek, and I recognized the gesture. *Where to begin*, it said. "We were in Reno."

And it got cold all of a sudden. We'd been hoboing around the country, and sort of got a taste for Nevada. Especially for gambling in Nevada. And hookers you knew wouldn't get you real sick, since it's legal. That was only if things had gone real well at the casino, though. It turned out that all the bad luck Bear had had in his life turned around when he sat at the blackjack table. There he was king. He was reckless too, though, so the trick was for me to drag him away from the table after he'd made, say five hundred dollars and wasn't too drunk yet. It was great to have the money, and gave us a break from panhandling, but it wasn't going to land us money for rent anywhere. Actually Bear did make five thousand one night but then lost it all trying to double it. It was beautiful though, when he was winning. The act of winning meant a lot to us because . . . just, I don't know. Anyway.

So we got caught up in Reno's casino scene and didn't make it south to Vegas like we planned before this brutal cold front hit. And later that week we were trying to sleep, huddled together like lovers just to survive against the weather, and Bear wakes me out up with this observation:

"Holy shit man, my dick's gonna freeze off."

"Yeah I know it's fucking cold, man, but stop bitching, you woke me up," I said.

"No dude, I literally cannot feel my dick." Bear jumped up and fumbled with his pants, his numb fingers frustrated by his button and zipper. "I have to see it," he said. "When I touch it it just feels like a piece of rock or something—but I don't have a boner for your ugly ass," he added, cutting off my wisecrack. He

got his pants down and moaned. "Oh no . . ." Bear's dick was an awful shade of blackish blue. If your dick was that color, you'd be freaking out too.

"I have to get to the clinic," he said. Which was a good mile and a half, two miles away.

"Yeah," I said. "You do."

During our miserable walk there somebody gave us a cup of hot coffee. Bear poured it down his pants right in front of the guy. For all I know, that's what saved his equipment. It was frostbite, and the doctor said he was lucky that Bear's member hadn't snapped right off, that it would have before much longer. So Bear made it to Las Vegas with his dick still attached.

Only . . . some tube or other in the inner workings must have froze shut and never quite worked the same again. Bear was completely impotent after that. Never got it up again. That's why, even If Bear was the kind to rape, which he was not, he never in the world would have tried.

I looked steadily at Jackson as he finished his story. "You know you are making things much more complicated."

"I do know that," he said. "It's worth it, because it's the truth."

I looked at the papers scattered across my desk, at the Ansel Adams pictures on the wall. There was no way out of it. "I'll reopen the case."

It wasn't because I was lazy that I dreaded looking further. It was just demoralizing. Good clean answers to crimes—especially the ugliest kinds of crime—were hard to come by. Even though I knew I had to look deeper, it was unlikely I'd find any answers.

I phoned my favorite deputy before stepping out. Gary Vasquez was a rising star in the department. Barely thirty, he hadn't become jaded and lazy but had been quick and intuitive beyond his years ever since joining the force. "Hi Gary," I said. "Please look deeper into every record you can find on Paul Conway, Isabelle Saroyan and Bob Espinoza."

"Can I ask why?" Gary said, sounding only mildly curious. An old codger like officer Wilson would have raged at such a waste of his time.

"I'll fill you in," I promised. "Just not right now."

I walked out the door and into the sunlight. Seagulls wheeled overhead, called from atop palm trees. Nothing like the iceland Jackson Comeau the wonderhobo had conjured up. Here I barely needed my suit coat. But I knew what it was to be cold. As I walked the sidewalk shifted to a different shade and texture, one that held a special place in my memory. It was February 1995, and I was in Chicago.

This would be, in the terms of that headline which gave me my fifteen minutes of fame, the HOMELESS part of my life. HERO was still many years and dead-end fast food jobs away. In Chicago the gray buildings stretched high above you, just as uncaring to the plight of a street-dweller in winter as the busy people who hurried by to their corporate meetings and skyscraper offices. The only companion I had back then was a black tabby named Midnight. I adopted her one night when I found her slinking around the same garbage can I was, just another stray. And it turned out more people tossed bills in your hat when you had a cute cat curled up in your lap. Even with cat food added to my budget, I had more money left over for beans, bread and the cheapest, most god-awful vodka ever to lurk inside a plastic bottle.

Or I did at first. The winter that year took a turn for the worse in a bad way. Just like Bear and Jackson, I'd been taking a little too much time getting to a better place. In my case, the better place was the homeless shelter. I'd been putting it off because I hated it there. There were too many people who'd been on the streets longer than their minds could take it, or probably they'd had a few marbles missing all along. The last time I'd slept in that cleaned-up warehouse, I'd woken up to a scabby toothless man massaging my crotch.

"Whatefer gez you off," he'd gargled from deep down a ruined throat. "I'll bwow you, you kin fuck me, jez gif me enof fer a little smack."

I was in no hurry to return to the shelter. When the blizzard hit I holed up in an alleyway. The alleyway became a hall with no door when the snow reached up two stories or more at the entrance. Some freak wind or a malicious God made it a high wall. The snowplows were too busy keeping roads and driveways clear to fuck with empty alleyways. I wasn't really trapped until it rained. The water froze over the snow, creating a slick hard barrier over the snow I could have maybe climbed over.

Midnight kept the claustrophobia away. Stroking her soft black pelt, stark against the whiteness everywhere, kept the panic of entombment away. She put off body heat I wouldn't reject either, huddled under my coats and blankets. If she was happy enough to purr at my touch, I could keep hopeful too. But I had more material needs, like hunger, and if Midnight found any frozen rats or pigeons, she kept them to herself.

At rock bottom I thought about how it'd all started, how I'd dropped out of community college to be a freewheeling hippie with my best friends, following whatever path the acid rainbow showed us. We had a VW bus (of course) that we ditched when we couldn't pay gas anymore. Some went back to the bourgeois life we'd sworn off when alternative living wasn't fun anymore. Some overdosed on drugs less playful than Lucy in the Sky with Diamonds. We had fun times, and we lived life exuberantly, we lived *more* than most people, but the journey frayed out eventually and now I found myself devoid of human friendship, starving in an Eskimo corridor. I thought of my mother more than anyone else.

Weeks passed. Hunger grew beyond what you and I are used to feeling. It became a raging animal in my stomach, a deep aching pain that inhibited my movement and clouded my thoughts. It was the voice of survival, of millions of years of evolution telling me to *find* something, *eat something*, just to stay alive. I kept sane by talking to Midnight, telling her how after this I really would escape my vagabond existence somehow, that she'd eat canned food in a kitchen and wear a name tag with an address on it. I told her I loved her as much as anyone ever loved a pet, but I must have been lying.

Four days before the snowplows busted me out I scratched Midnight behind the ears one last time and then snapped her neck. I ate my best friend. Bitter tears rolled down my cheeks into my beard, even as it was all I could do to eat the raw meat slowly, to not shock my stomach into rejecting its only sustenance in weeks. That waste would have been unthinkable.

I shook myself out of my reverie. I had almost reached my destination, and Winthrop the Absent-Minded Detective wasn't really the street rep I was going for. CHURCHILL PARK the faded metal sign announced as I entered the glorified expansion of lawn and picnic tables. As is so often the case with official names, the dignified label CHURCHILL was irrelevant and hopelessly out of date to everyone in Santa Roma county who knew the place as Speed Market Park or sometimes Tramp Row. A group of seven or eight vagabonds lounged at a table in one of the few areas of shade afforded by an oak tree. The trees kept their distance from one another like shy guests at a party they'd never wanted to come to.

"Hi fellas," I called as I approached. "Got a minute?"

"Naw," a familiar face replied. "I've got to run to keep an appointment with my stock broker."

I laughed and clasped hands with the man. Oliver Stamp, a hobo I used to know who was mainly kept on the street by his expensive tastes. I introduced myself to the others, a scowling dark-skinned man with a mohawk, a woman who was easily the hottest young thing I'd seen without a home—with her modest foundation of dust and her long dreadlocks, she could have jumped from the pages of a fashion magazine doing a don't-give-a-shit style photo shoot. Another man snored on the ground, peacefully oblivious to the intruding fuzz, and an ancient looking woman gazed at me with the rest of them. She was dressed in an enormous puffy pink dress, a towering, colorful hat and purple and green makeup which added a gypsy flair to her wrinkles.

"I wanted to know if any of you knew this man," I said, and pulled out a picture of Robert Espinoza.

"Bear!" Oliver said at once. "He came by every once in a while. He wasn't exactly a member of the family, but great guy."

"We know he's dead," Mohawk said angrily, as though I'd killed him myself.

"Yes," I said. "I thought you'd know, and I was hoping you might know more than that. Would you describe Bear as . . . as someone who liked to chase a skirt?"

"Was he horny?" Oliver smirked.

"Fuck no," the dreadlocked girl said. Her voice was as husky as a smoker twice her age and did nothing to hurt her salacious effect. "Bear's the only bum I know who's never hit on me."

"Okay," I said. "Now, was Bear involved in anything unusual? Especially very recently leading up to his death?"

The pink lady with the hat looked around at the others.

"Winthrop's alright," Oliver assured her. I made a mental note to put in a good word for him with the homeless organizations and job outreach programs.

Pink looked at me with wide eyes. "I saw Bear a week before he died," she said in a little grandma voice. "But, he didn't see *me*."

I nodded.

"I was reading under a streetlight—it was night time, and he met up with this clean cut-looking guy across the street. That boy was *nervous*, he kept looking around, but there was nobody around but us, and I don't think he even saw me. I blend in, you know." She winked at me. "So I was sure Bear must be selling, well, *drugs*—especially because that other man gave Bear some money. But I never saw Bear give him anything—maybe he *did*, but I didn't *see* it, you understand." She inclined her head at me and raised her eyebrows.

"I understand, ma'am," I said.

"Good," she said, "because here's the most important part. That other man pulled out a *gun*, a, a, a *pistol*, and my *Lord*, my heart just leaped up into my throat then, but the man just gave it to Bear and walked off."

"I'm sorry, ma'am," I said. "I don't think I caught your name?"

"It's Alice, sweetheart," she said. "And I don't believe in last names anymore, so Alice will have to do."

"That's just fine, Alice. Can you describe the man who met with Bear as best you can?"

"Well, he was pretty average, I'm sorry to tell you. He was white, about average height—it was dark, so I don't know if his hair was blonde or brown, but it wasn't black."

"Not pink?" I smiled.

"No. Smart aleck."

I sat down across from Gary Vasquez in our cluttered office. The sun was going down, casting amber lines through the blinds on our wooden bookshelves.

"Someone," I told Gary, "paid Bob 'Bear' Espinoza to attack Paul and Isabel."

"Damn," he said. I related the story Alice had told me.

"So," I continued, "when you were looking into their personal histories, did you find anyone who could have been an enemy of either of them?"

"Not an enemy, per se," Gary said. "But Paul Conway has had some pretty unfortunate experiences in his life." He pulled out some pages with lines highlighted in green. "He grew up in Daytona, Florida. There's only one legal incident that made it into his records, but it's a doozy." He flipped through a couple pages.

"When Paul was 18, he went to a party with his sister . . ." he scanned the page. "Amy. There was plenty of underage drinking, pretty typical stuff. But his sister, Amy, was raped at the party. They reported it, and that's how we know all the details, and three guys went to prison."

"Hoo," I said.

He read my expression. "No, not a gang-rape. The other two were accomplices. It seems that Paul burst in and attempted to defend his sister, and that's where the other two guys came into the picture. They held him . . . and they made him watch."

"Christ."

"Yeah." Gary smiled sadly. "With that kind of history, I'm surprised he only shot Espinoza once."

I reached under my desk for the whiskey I'd served Paul Conway and pulled out two glasses with it. Gary nodded his head appreciatively and continued.

"Neither Paul or Amy stayed anywhere near home. Amy went to New York; Paul bounced around the Bay area before settling here in Santa Roma.

"So—that leaves Isabelle and Bob Espinoza. Isabelle grew up in the area; the only thing on her record is running a red light in 2005. Espinoza has the usual checklist of petty crime that come with being homeless . . ." his eyes flickered up at mine and I waved a hand in an *of course* gesture and set down his glass of whiskey to indicate I wasn't offended.

"Vagrancy, trespassing, petty theft, public drunkenness. This week was the first time he'd committed a felony. Aaand that's all Uncle Sam's got on 'em," he concluded. He rewarded his account with a sip of Jameson's.

I was still thinking of what had happened to Amy Conway back in Daytona. Sometimes I hated my job. Every crime I was supposed to somehow rectify took another bite out of my faith in the human race. Every time I thought I'd seen it all, I was surprised by some new act of cruelty—like forcing a man to watch his sister's rape. Back when I was young and idealistic—and yes, called a VW bus my home, I'd honestly felt like I was a part of humanity. But humanity had become alien. I felt myself becoming more and more of a parody of the noveau detective, jaded, cynical and world-weary.

I took a healthy swig from my own glass. "When someone does something really brutal," I said, resting my jaw on my propped fist, "people say: 'What an animal.' But people should be more like animals. More like . . . cats. Cats don't rape each other."

"Actually," said Gary Vasquez, "Not to burst your bubble, I like lolcats as much as anyone, but cats have barbs on the ends of their dicks. So the girl cat can't get away."

What a world.

Gary took another drink and performed a fascinating facial expression. It began as a whiskey-fueled grimace and then morphed into a look of surprise. "I almost forgot!" he said. "The whiskey reminded me—there is one other thing about Paul Conway. He drinks at the same bar I go to on Friday nights—Srinu's."

A week passed, and I was standing outside the police department smoking a Pall Mall and soaking up the sun. Santa Roma is the beneficiary of California's sunny reputation sometimes, but Northern California gets as much rain as anywhere else in the winter months, so I cherished the sun in the summer. *Pho-to-synthesis, pho-to-synthesis*, I thought in a squeaky Spongebob voice. You think cops don't watch cartoons? Spongebob is prime television when you're drunk.

A familiar face walked up. Jackson Comeau, with his frayed but remarkably clean black hair. Maybe he took a skinny-dip in the river in the morning, and let the water carry his homeless grime the short distance to the ocean.

"Hi Jackson," I said, and offered him a cigarette. He waved it away.

"Hi detective," he said. "I came to see if there was anything new in Bear's case.

I leaned against the stoop's railing.

"I'm sorry to say there isn't, other than the homeless community confirming what you said about his character."

"Oh," he said. The smile dropped from his face. "So that's it?"

"'Fraid so."

"A man has been murdered and that's it."

I took a fresh glance at his face. It was outwardly calm, but I sensed anger lurking beneath the surface.

I put a hand on his shoulder. "Jackson," I said. "I'm so sorry for the loss of your friend. There's just no leads, no witnesses, no nothing."

"What about the man who killed him?"

"The man who killed him has never been on anything but the victim side of a crime. No record, no reason to believe this was anything but an accident."

Jackson smacked my hand away. "And what's it matter anyway?" he said. "One less *bum* for the city to worry about cussing out the tourists?" He spat the word.

"The police don't discriminate—"

"Bullshit." Jackson voice rose to a quavery almost-yell. "You're going to stand there and tell me if this was a store-owner or college student from up the hill got shot, it'd be case closed, we believe the assailant? Bullshit. Horse shit." He eyed my badge contemptuously. "*Pig* shit."

A cop coming up the steps into the building hesitated, his hand dropping to the butt of his gun before going in.

"Look—" I started.

"No," Jackson shouted. He was on a roll. "I expected better from you, Winthrop. You're as bad as the rest. You're worse. You're what my black friends would call an Uncle Tom, but this time it's the cabin you can go home to that matters."

Homeless folk read. They've got time for it, and used books are cheap.

Jackson raised a finger to my face. Kids at the bus stop across the street stared at the cop being harangued by a ragged street man. "You're disgusting. I hope you wind up back on the street, and ain't none of us going to give you an ounce of help. You burn in—"

"*Hey!*" I shouted, lowering my voice and letting it come from my stomach the way we had been trained. "You forget you are talking to an officer of the law. I will not be spoken to that way."

"Fuck you," he muttered, but the fight had gone out of him.

"Get out of here," I said. "Before I arrest you."

I went inside, my mouth suddenly flooded with the taste of raw cat. Warm and bloody, I could even feel the hair on my tongue.

I told myself I didn't care what Jackson thought of me. I told myself that had nothing to do with deciding to call Paul Conway and Isabelle Saroyan in for second interviews. That was useless, as my colleagues knew it would be. They couldn't believe I was wasting time on the matter when several robberies and an increasingly wrought protest movement on the college campus had occurred since the shooting. Isabelle's story matched Paul's perfectly, and he told the same story as before. Paul looked bad. There were bags under his eyes and the beginnings of an ugly neck beard. They couldn't think of anyone who'd want to hurt them. Even their jealous exes were well-adjusted and well-behaved.

Truth was, I believed them. I believed Jackson too, other than his unflattering character assessment of yours truly. A good man can do bad things. I imagined that Bear's impotency caused him great frustration on top of an already difficult life, and when he was offered money to kill Paul, his moral character had taken too many hits to put up much of a fight. Maybe he'd had one too many drinks the night he agreed to it.

Incidentally, that was exactly how much I wanted to drink the night I went to Srinu's.

Srinu's was a place on the corner of Smalley and Myrtle downtown. The location was great, the bar itself so tiny first-timers on their way to meet somebody regularly walked past it at first. I ducked in because bartenders hear a lot of stories—also because I didn't have anything better to do.

"Hi Srinu," I said as he plunked my beer down.

"That's on the house, blue," he said. An optimist would have called the establishment half-crowded that evening, which gave Srinu the freedom to shoot the shit with me. The bar-keep was an Indian man with a dark mustache of which I was deeply jealous. He wore a cap bearing the legend IT'S 5 O'CLOCK SOMEWHERE!

"How's your novel coming?" I asked him.

"Slow as molasses," he said. "I'm halfway done with the second draft, and if I had a time machine I'd go back and kick my own ass for writing the first draft by hand. But you know, I used to worry that the thing was too melodramatic—that was before I got my job bartending. My story's love triangle looks like a Mennonite courtship compared to the issues these people have." He flickered his eyes around the bar to indicate his customers. "Are the ladies biting, Winthrop?"

It occurred to me that my love life must be my project comparable to Srinu's novel. The kind of man who talks to cats is the kind of man who will bitch about the fickleness of women to his bartender, sometimes even drunkenly wax poetic about the pain of a broken heart. I'd be embarrassed about it if Srinu weren't such quality people, as my hippie friends would have called him.

"Nah. Met a cute girl today but she's homeless. You want to talk about issues." Now I looked around the bar. There were a few women present, but they were mostly cougar types. I'd be flattered if they talked to me, it'd be like being carded.

"My friend Gary Vasquez told me Paul Conway drinks here. Has he been okay since his run-in with a mugger?"

"Is that what happened to him?" He saw my eyebrows reaching for the ceiling and added: "Mum's the word, I know. No. He has definitely not been okay."

"What do you mean?"

"He came in the other night, already coked out and liquored up. He was talking to me nonstop, but I couldn't understand what he was saying. Poor guy."

"What kinds of things was he saying?" Maybe I asked that in my detective Winthrop voice or something; it seemed like Srinu sensed I wasn't asking for the sake of gossip. He frowned, remembering.

"'It wasn't supposed to happen,' he said a lot, and variants around that, like 'it wasn't supposed to happen like that,' and 'it wasn't supposed to go so far.' Those he said over and over again. At one bad point I had to stop him beating his head against the bar while he said it.

"I took him around to the back of the bar then, because as you can imagine he was starting to make a scene. It's just a little storage room back there, barely big enough for him and I to fit, but better than nothing. Paul calmed down. He started to tell me about this bum he'd met doing volunteer stuff at the soup kitchen. I guess his girlfriend is really into volunteering. So he was talking about how this bum was the nicest guy he'd ever met, and that it was such a shame he lived a rough life, and I guess this guy had told him he wished he had more protection or something, or had been roughed up a few times. Paul said he was going to give the guy his old gun, or already had, or something.

"Then he got a little weepy and said he thought they'd each be able to do the other a favor. After that he went back from making little sense to making no sense. He mentioned his sister, and said something wonky like: "you always want to atone, but you can't atone, you're not a stone, you're made of bone." Drunk stuff. I don't know. He left after that. He said one more really weird thing. I said, "Goodnight Paul, take care of yourself."

Someone down the bar called for a drink. Srinu turned and held up a finger: *just a minute*. His mouth was a flat line.

"He looked back at me with the door held open, half in, half out. 'It's not Paul,' he said. 'It's Saul.'"

I left Srinu watering cougars and went home deep in thought. I remembered Paul Conway in my office just two nights ago, and saw him the way Alice had seen him, a very average young man with average light brown hair. I don't know who he was trying to prove himself to that night: his sister, his girlfriend—probably just himself, underneath it all. But things got out of hand. I wondered which idiot had loaded the gun, Paul or Bear. I wondered whether there was any point or duty in arresting Paul. I sure didn't want to.

If I'd stayed at Srinu's a couple hours longer I would have seen Paul himself when he showed up around one. Srinu told me the whole story later.

Paul didn't waste any time. Almost as soon as he got there he followed Big Andy Kush and his girl outside. Andrew Jacob Kush is the baddest fish in the little pond of Santa Roma, a man who's served some jail time, but has mostly gotten away with his acts as the ringleader of the region's interlocking drug rings—acts like murder. He's an enormous black man with a wolf paw print tattooed on the side of his shaved head.

Big Andy paused under a streetlight outside to pull out a couple cigarettes. His girlfriend was one of those types who are petite generally and far from petite in certain places. Her breasts spilled over her halter top and her ass swelled as though trying to escape from her tiny shorts, S-E-X-Y printed across the backside. Big Andy was extending a lighter to the Marlboro jutting from her lips when Paul snatched an arm around her neck and pulled her backwards. She screamed, and the small crowd that permanently milled outside the bar turned in collective agitation to see.

Paul pulled out a tiny red pocket knife and held it to her throat. "This cocktease is coming with me!" he shouted. He stood to her side, a clear gap between their bodies. He looked like an over-enthused escort at the prom. Her throat worked violently and her eyes darted to Big Andy.

Big Andy pulled out a pistol with a barrel long enough he probably used it to scratch that hard-to-reach spot on his sizable back.

"Let go of my woman," he said.

Paul screamed: "I'm gonna fill every hole she's got!" and stepped further away from her. Big Andy fired four times. Four sprays of blood exploded from Paul's back. The crowd screamed. Paul lay dead on the sidewalk. Unknowingly, Big Andy had perfectly fulfilled the role Paul had intended for him.

Life is a wheel, to paraphrase my favorite author, Stephen King. Life is a wheel, and you will find situations repeating themselves in your life as the big wheel makes another revolution. When the wheel came full circle on Paul Conway, he tried to roll it the other way, and rode it straight to his death. All we can do is recognize when our wheels are rolling in a place we've been before, and try to do a little better than last time.

That's what I'm doing, and it's about time I got a new cat.

THE WISH-GRANTER

Every night we meet at the road overlooking the bay. We stand away from
the streetlights, away from the lighthouse with its circling beams. The
ocean looks different by unadulterated moonlight. The jutting cliffs on
the side of the road look different, and the oaks that peer over the edge,
their leaves shimmering like stars that fall to the waves below. Sometimes
the ocean is violent, and beats against the cliff as if to take us, its spray
reaching up to try to touch us. Sometimes the ocean lies almost flat, and
the moon and its reflection make eyes on a face that's lying down, and the
rolls in the water too still to break are like breaths over a pillow.

We didn't always stand in a group overlooking the bay. I started
running along the cliffside when _____ broke my heart. Gradually I
realized how much the run was beginning to mean to me. It had to be at
night, especially late at night when the moon had risen high in the sky. In
the day the cliffside road was clogged with surfers, bicyclists and runners,
often pushing a stroller or accompanied by a dog or two. But at night the
streets were quiet, almost deserted. The place itself was allowed to emerge,
and it was easy to notice the subtleties of the stairway into the water, the
grass on the other side of the cliff's railing, the statue of the angel on the
church and the statue of the surfer off the sidewalk.

At first I was nervous about running at night. Santa Roma has its
fair share of crime, and everyone told me I was asking to get mugged.
But one night I came back from running to find that my apartment had
been burglarized while I was gone. After that I rethought my ideas about
whether I was more secure outside or at home.

My initial jumpiness made me wary of anyone else on the streets that
time of night—anywhere from ten to three o' clock. One night I'd tagged
the lighthouse and was on my way back, walking, because I rarely ran the

whole way, when a figure with his sweatshirt hood pulled over his head reversed his own steps to approach me.

"Nice night, isn't it?" I called, wondering if this was the night I'd be attacked.

"Very nice," he replied softly, the distance closing between us. "Are you running?"

"Yeah," I said. I stopped and waited at the side of the cliff's railing.

""Did I scare you?" he asked with a heavy Mexican accent. He smiled at my tense posture.

"A little," I said.

"I'm just running too," he said, and made the peace sign. "Don't worry."

He left me to wonder guiltily if I'd been racist in my reaction to him. Now I see Alejandro almost every night, in our own little lonely hearts club band.

You see, after a while I came to notice I wasn't the only one drawn to the cliffside at night. There were always a few people at the more scenic parts of the road, sometimes parked at the little lot between the surfer statue and the lighthouse, often leaning on the railing, smoking a cigarette and peering over the sea, or perhaps waiting to sell or buy some drugs. Nights when the moon is full are when the most of us are drawn out. We've come to sense our commonality, which is best represented by the boardwalk that frames the left side of our bay's panorama from our vantage point. The boardwalk is Santa Roma's tourist attraction, and in the summer it's a source of noise and brightness, music and the screams of people on rollercoasters. It's alive with the laughing innocence of children and the burning lust of teenagers in board shorts and bikinis. Even into the beginning of the night it lights up the beach with thousands of bulbs along its rides and shops.

But later, when we come out to look over the bay the boardwalk is empty, its silence somehow deepened by the ghosts of all its daytime noise. It is missing something, as we who listen to the waves at night are all missing something.

It was an old homeless man who I like to call Gandalf for his long beard and funny hat with shells tied to the brim who brought us together. Some people say Gandalf is a mystic, and others say he's crazy, which I think is like arguing over the right way to pronounce ketchup.

One night I was feeling less antisocial than usual and paused alongside the railing by the little lot. My ankles hurt, so I planted one set of toes on the ground at a time and circled my feet around. I nodded at the man standing a few yards away and he returned the silent greeting, grateful, I think, that I hadn't tried to initiate conversation. I was happy that there were no couples gazing at the sea with their arms linked around each other. It wasn't until later that I realized that although I often ran by couples on a moonlit walk, they were not among those who stayed for hours at a time, as though waiting for the water to give them an answer to something important. Lovers were antithetical to this place, to that behavior.

On my left a ragged, bearded figure shuffled towards me and I felt a pang of irritation. I had my response ready: *I don't have any money on me.*

But instead Gandalf said: "The sea grants wishes."

"Oh yeah?" I answered with polite interest.

"The sea still grants wishes. But she is always dangerous."

"That's for sure," I agreed.

The man on my right turned toward us and leaned an elbow on the railing. "'The sea grants wishes.' That's nice." He spoke with a good-natured roughness I associated more with my small town back home than with this college town. "That sounds like something in a picture book I would have read to my daughter." The man's voice turned rough suddenly at the word *daughter*, and he turned back to dig a cigarette out of his breast pocket.

Our words hung in the air, suspended by the regular crashing of the waves. There was no uncomfortableness, no compulsion to continue the conversation further. The waves came again and again, their sound which never really ended but simply rose and fell in endless quiet crescendos like the ticking of a more natural clock, marked a different kind of time. After some unknowable number of waves I came out of my reverie and the desire came to go home and sleep.

"I'm Peter," I told them before I went.

"Richard," the other man said, and lifted a hand in farewell from where he leaned. There was, again, a sense of perfect understanding that a handshake would have been superfluous. I turned to the homeless man, who only smiled at me serenely.

"Anyone ever call you Gandalf?" I asked.

"What's in a name?" he said.

Well, I'd studied the useless discipline of literature in my college days, and though I'd never gotten the degree, I knew where that little ditty came from. *A rose by any other name would smell as sweet*, says Juliet to her lover.

"You're a rose, my friend, it's true," I said.

It got to be so there were ten of us out there some nights, and there were always at least three or four. Mostly men, but there were a few women. None of us were as old we looked, even in the dark, even the ones who were old. I'd noticed my own wrinkles setting in more firmly under my eyes and tracing from the sides of my nose to the corners of my mouth, decades before they were due. The embers of our cigarettes formed red, ragtag constellations, the damage they did our lungs irrelevant to our deeper injuries.

We spoke in short intervals, never about ourselves. We never said *how are you*, and so we were completely honest in our exchanges. The comfort we gave each other was never more explicit than a brief touch on the shoulder. It was insufficient medicine, and about that, too, we were honest. The bay was where we shed the faces we put on for society.

On nights when the sea was flat, I drifted so far into myself I forgot anyone was there with me. On those nights the sea resembled a vast, unending field under the moonlight. It looked like the meadow back home in the foothills where I'd lain with _____, where I'd set down a blanket and taken her virginity as the stars shone down on us, so much more numerous than here, where the city lights choked them out.

I guess it was almost a month ago now that I sat through the night with Gandalf. I'd gone up the road a little ways, where the drop is higher and the rocks at the bottom twist the waves up in the air when they come in. I'd come to that place, that night, because I was tired of going back and forth in my head, tired of putting off the decision until later. That was the night I'd stay as long as I needed to decide whether to end my life then, or never. I stared down at the rocks, confident they'd do the job if I asked it of them, going through all the arguments over and over.

Soon Gandalf showed up and parked it a few yards away from me. A respectable distance, and he never said a word. Though I'd needed solitude, his presence didn't bother me as much as anyone else's would have. Somehow I sensed that should I choose the exit, I could do it in front of him without worrying about his feelings, and that he wouldn't try to stop me.

So I stared down at the waves and eddies, and after a while their constant motion became a kind of stillness, a rhythm I wasn't any more conscious of than my heartbeat or my breath. Each point lead to a counterpoint, the same ones that have fought each other in anyone's head who's ever thought about whether it all might be better to throw in the towel. My mother will be devastated. I can't live for my mother. Life might get better. And it might not. And it might not be worth waiting for even so. And so on. The endless ebb and flow of the tide, each wave begetting another pull back.

Every once it a while I'd look over to my left and Gandalf would still be there, soundless, motionless, looking out over the waves. The moon trekked across the sky. I stood at the edge of the cliff, my legs always ready for that last command from the control panel up top: *jump*. Eventually I became conscious that the horizon was brightening. My night of contemplation was drawing to a close; the time to decide was coming very close.

I looked back at Gandalf one last time, and he spoke for the first time throughout that long cold night. "Sun and moon make *soon*," he said in his old man's voice.

"What?"

"Sun and moon," he said, enunciating as though that was why I hadn't understood him, "make *soon*."

"Crazy," I muttered, and turned back to the bay, and the sun rose. It started as a tiny bump on the horizon, but rose and became brighter and brighter until it was the sun you'd always known, the one that hurt to look at because it was no longer pink, no longer orange, but all burning, shining white. It lit the water up, lit up the whitecaps on the deep blue, lit up all the golden brown cliffs and the gulls and pelicans wheeling in the air, brought song from all the birds that didn't fish from the ocean but didn't mind nesting in the trees along its shores and I was crying but didn't know it and then I knew it and I looked back at Gandalf because I didn't know what to do with all the awful beauty all on my own but Gandalf was gone. So I picked myself up and went home and fried some eggs.

The first time I went to the cliffside in the pouring rain I was sure I'd be the only one there. But if anything, more people felt drawn to the outlook than ever. Cigarettes burned under umbrellas that shuddered under the weight of the constant downpour, and sometimes a joint or a glass pipe would glow as well. Sometimes the glass pipe was mine. Then there were people who came without umbrellas, letting the rain batter them as though hoping to drown.

It was on such a night that I walked the dark streets to the bay and noticed that something seemed a little different, a little off-kilter—the kind of thing you couldn't quite put your finger on. Then I came to the streetlight before our meeting place and stared. The surfer statue was gone from his post. The stone block where he usually stood, manly chest jutting out as he gripped his board behind him, was deserted. The missing landmark left me with a lost feeling, as though I'd accidentally found myself on some other cliffside.

I came to the group was lined along the rail. I saw Gandalf's hat jutting above the others' heads. There was Katy, a woman with gray straight hair, and Eddie among them. Eddie was the only figure who evoked pity in the rest of us, I think. Call us selfish, but we all recognized in each other our own pain, and experienced more a feeling of solidarity than sympathy. It was just that Eddie was so *young*. Thirteen, tops, but I'd guess more like ten. He always wore a black sweatshirt with the tip of his hair just poking out from the hood.

I'd been there sharing the silence for ten minutes or so when Eddie saw it. "Someone is *surfing!*" he exclaimed, raising an arm and pointing. And someone was, at midnight in the middle of the storm. When the beams of the lighthouse swung over the figure, we saw the rest of the picture. Again, it was Eddie who voiced what we all saw, perhaps because he was too young for the idea of what was impossible to be firmly settled in his mind. "It's the *statue!*"

The tall gray figure stood straight up on his board as it zipped and hooked along the waves. Its body was unnaturally still, not twisting and crouching the way surfers do. It shouldn't have been able to keep its balance like that, but it was.

"What in the hell did I smoke tonight?" asked Richard, and we all laughed the giggly laughs of those under strain. We were seeing an impossibility, but there was no denying what our eyes saw. The rain fell hard, but not thick enough to obscure the reality of the man made of granite navigating the surf just as though he shouldn't have sunk to the bottom of the sea like the rock he was.

As we watched, the figure raised an arm. And waved. *Come on in, the water's fine.*

Gandalf spoke in the tone of a man who is an authority on a certain subject of knowledge. "The sea is awake tonight." Drops of rain dripped from the end of his beard. "And may grant favors. What has been lost, may be found again."

There was a silence, during which all our minds struggled to comprehend the magnitude of his words. For we were all of us souls who had lost something.

I thought of _____, who I would always love, and always in vain. Since she'd left, I'd brought home women from bars that were better in bed in ways that had everything to do with my cock, and nothing to do with my heart and the way it swelled when _____ whispered my name into the cup of my ear when I was inside her. And whispered that she loved me. I would do anything to go back in time to when she still loved me. I'd do everything differently and treat her the way she deserved. I'd do anything for that second chance.

For I'd been stupid and taken her for granted when she was mine. People are foolish like that. If you look at the brightest jewel every day, it's possible to forget how dull everything is without its shine; to not realize how much light it brings to your existence.

It was Richard, the man who'd lost his daughter, who spoke for us. "What do we have to do?"

It was the right question, for none of us doubted Gandalf's words. We had only to look at the man riding the waves on a board that couldn't float to know that reality was thinner than we'd ever imagined, and that to doubt now was to lose everything a second time.

We made our way down a staircase to the waves. With each step down, the storm seemed to intensify. Sea lions were barking on some nearby rock peninsula. I couldn't tell you when they had begun barking, in the way you never know when you first notice background noise, but I sure as hell noticed now. Their barks grew louder and louder until it was cacophonous, frenzied like a pack of wild dogs or coyotes, each striving to outdo the rest.

I turned a corner and a beam from the lighthouse blinded me. Its revolving light spun at an insane speed, creating a strobe light effect as we groped our way to the water, shielding our faces against the rain that gusted sideways against us. We might as well have already been in the ocean.

When we reached the bottom of the stairs we clambered over the slippery rocks, and finally, into the sea itself. That was the moment I felt silly, standing in chest-deep freezing water with half a dozen others. We bobbed and treaded water when waves rolled at us, but the ocean itself was intensifying with the storm. Then I didn't have the luxury of feeling silly.

The waves crashed back at us from the rocks and the cliff face, so that they seemed to come from every direction.

A brief respite from the waves came, and I felt a powerful pull around my legs and waist. The water level drained before our eyes, and then we saw what the riptide was creating. The wave was enormous, towering. I saw my companions wrap their arms around rocks, bracing themselves, and then it smashed down on us.

All the noise of the storm and the sea lions was snuffed out. The wave drove me headfirst into a rock, and I gasped in seawater. Instantly a deep pain erupted in my chest, and I coughed involuntarily, but I was still underwater and only sucked in more. The tide pulled me out further and the crashing waves on the surface churned and spun me as I tried to swim up in panic. But I was wearing shoes and couldn't tell if my strokes made any headway against the elements. I couldn't expel the water from my lungs, and it *burned* and it was *heavy*. My flailing arms struck something hard and I scrabbled madly at it. Oh thank Christ, it was dry, and I felt *air*, and heaved myself from the water onto the flat rock. I heaved, and at first I was still unable to dispel the water and breathe air. I vomited, and all the while I felt terror, because I vomited out water, but I still wasn't *breathing*, and even as my stomach forced burning salt *out* I was desperately trying to breathe in. Then I was coughing, and in between my coughs out snatched tiny inhalations that weren't enough, weren't even *close* to enough, and then finally I drew in a deep, racking breath that hurt my chest like hell, but I was breathing again, and I wasn't drowning anymore, wasn't dying anymore in a huge, enveloping murderous tomb. I curled up on my side and coughed, and waited for the pain to go away.

Finally I sat up and took in my surroundings. I was in a kind of cove. The rock floor was smooth from years of erosion, and the ceiling domed about fifteen feet overhead. Stubby beginnings of stalactites hung from its top. It took me less than a minute to walk to the back, where the tiny cave ended. Turning back, I saw waves lapping mildly at the floor's lip, almost like it was a ramp into a swimming pool. I began to think about swimming out, but was in no hurry to return to the stormy water. Then I saw a large dark shape under the surface. *Shark*, I thought instantly, and looked fearfully for the telltale dorsal fin. The shape came closer to the edge of the cove. Not a shark then, after all, it was too wide, somehow.

Part of the thing surfaced. It was a giant manta ray, its body sleek and flat and spread out into wings. I took a step back as, contrary to biology, the animal rose onto the land and raised itself to a vertical position.

"Peter Kiedis." I looked for anyone, anything in the cove but this creature, but it seemed undeniable the thing itself was talking. It spoke in the sound of crushed seashells underfoot.

"Yes," I said, and it was almost a question.

"You may earn back the one you love," it said.

My heart jumped in my throat. It seemed to beat faster even than when I was drowning, and I felt a delirious emotion that had been absent for years: hope. Wild, afraid-to-believe hope.

"Do you promise?" I asked, my voice sounding strange to my own ears.

"The ocean makes no promises. You will make it to the other side, or the ocean will devour you, for the ocean is always hungry."

I stared up at the ray's underbelly. It looked much creepier seen from this angle, not the animal that was almost cute seen from above or the side. I looked at the slits that made its gills and mouth, at its horn-like lobes. It did not escape me that this was the animal sailors used to call the devil fish.

"All right," I said, then hesitated, and added: "Thank you."

"Swim," the ray said. It slipped back into the water and was gone.

I stripped off my clothes and left them in a sopping pile. I was warmer without them. I dove into the water. It was calm as I swam freestyle out of the cove into the wider sea, and then the ocean pummeled me. I struggled to stay on the surface. Again and again a wave would crash down on me, pushing me under, and I would paddle back, exhaling great bubbles as I neared the surface and then gasping in another lungful before the next wave hit me.

It was a struggle I was doomed to lose. A wave ambushed me from behind, and flipped me over underwater. I felt burning water gush up my nose, and fought the urge to cough. I pushed the water around me in quick, wide breast strokes, but I could no longer tell which way was up. I prayed to a God I didn't quite believe in that I wasn't only swimming further down, and forced myself to stop swimming altogether, to look for some sign of the surface, or to see if I could feel myself float up. It was useless, and the air in my lungs began to grow hot, stale and burning. I was terrified of repeating the experience I had so narrowly escaped, but I knew that in a few more minutes the feeling of suffocation would become so desperate and overpowering that I would be helpless not to breathe in water. And this time, it would kill me.

I swam again, blindly trusting my sense of direction. My foot kicked against something long and narrow that seemed too thick to be seaweed. I could feel my strokes pushing water back from me, but had no way of knowing if I was even moving at all. The thought occurred to me that the tide could be pulling me backwards and I wouldn't even know, and I shoved it aside before it could panic me any further.

Suddenly I heard Gandalf's voice clearly in my head. *Sun and moon make soon.* Something glimmered in the corner of my eye. There in the distance, at what I'd thought was my side, was unmistakable daylight shining through the water. I swam for it. Closer, and closer, the poisoned air in my lungs screaming to be spewed out and replaced.

Something wrapped around my leg. I knew it was the tentacle I'd kicked before. I let out a scream, precious life-giving bubbles escaping my lips and stealing my buoyancy. I wrenched my leg free and swam on. So close now. I saw an arm reaching down into the water where the sun shone in. It was _____'s arm, I knew it even seeing it underwater. Then the tentacle squeezed around my leg again, wrapping itself up to my thigh. I felt dozens of suckers bite into me as it yanked me down.

I kicked down with my other leg and connected with something like a half-deflated basketball. It was yielding, but firm underneath. I stroked upward with all my strength, the thing holding me like an anchor, stretched out an arm and caught _____'s hand. I held onto it as the thing below me pulled, and I felt my limbs stretching in their sockets. Then my love pulled me free, and I burst out into the daylight.

WHAT?

Wheel-wong
the wind swings
Sing-song
the fish breathes
and the coconuts lay
restfully.

Pring-prong
the wheel reads
Gang-gong
the road speeds
and the crocodiles smile
listlessly.

Bang-bong
the boys sneeze
Right-wrong
the girls heave
and the clouds meditate
blissfully.

Fing-fong
the mist weaves
Tang-tong
the ink pleads
and the cable cars stop
fecklessly.

"LARPing Gets You Laid, Says Surprised Nerd"—
The Fish Rap Live! January 2011

FRL! was contacted late Friday night by a student excited to have lost his virginity. Shockingly, Ernest Octavio is not only a member of the live action role playing community, seen often swinging foam swords at one another and yelling, "No I hit you," but attributes his carnal success to LARPing itself.

"Engaging in epic battles against the rival hordes was always a way for me to work out my sexual frustration," said Octavio, a third-year from Crown College. "I never dreamed that, like Parcival and the knights of old, my heroics would win me a maiden of mine own!"

Octavio was fiercely protective of the identity of said maiden. "She made it very clear she didn't want people to know we had been together. I think that's romantic."

However, subsequent investigation revealed the girl's identity as Clara Fishborne, one of the few women to participate in LARPing.

"It was Clara," said fellow LARPer Heinrich Olbermunde. "Total skank. And she swings a mace like a plague-ridden squire."

Olbermunde denied that jealousy motivated his negative feelings toward Fishborne. "I could be up to my codpiece in chicks, but I happen to adhere to a code of chivalry which *some* people appear to have forgotten."

Sixth-year Percy Whittingfield, general of the Greater Saxon Alliance, agreed that sexual activity among his soldiers has become a problem.

"Octavio is not an isolated case," he said. "Many recruits who had previously retained all their energy for the cause are now carelessly depleting their hot oil reserves on wenches."

Indeed, desertion has become more of a problem among LARP troops, as greater numbers of students choose sex over being hit in the face with giant blue lances.

"There may be only one way to settle this," said Whittingfield, fingering the edge of a polyurethane battle axe. "I speak of war."

Fishborne was hard-pressed to explain the attraction she had for Octavio as she watched him running around a field swinging a sword and reciting Monty Python lines at the top of his lungs.

"I mean," she said, "it beats lacrosse players."

"Joe Biden, Michelle Bachman go on V-Day Lunch Date"—The Fish Rap Live! February 2011

Drawing on the popular move last month to have Congressional Democrats and Republicans sit together for the President's State of the Union speech, Vice President Joe Biden and Congresswoman Michelle Bachman went out for a Valentine's Day lunch date in the new spirit of bipartisanism.

"Everything was going pretty well until I went and put my foot in my mouth again," admitted Biden with a winning grin. According to sources at the upscale restaurant in the D.C. area, Biden told Bachman that she wasn't so bad for being a succubus fueled by the undead rage of Joe McCarthy.

Things smoothed over when the pair ordered drinks. Biden had a straight Hennessy cognac and Bachman ordered her signature brew of absinthe, Krista discount vodka and two shots of horse tranquilizer. The two bonded over their shared hatred of the Democratic base.

"Everything that has gone wrong in the administration," Biden confided to the Republican from Minnesota, "is the damn liberal bloggers' fault. They are never satisfied with anything. I mean, giving a shit about Guantanamo Bay is *so* 2007."

Bachman agreed. "Don't they realize that forcing people to buy health care from corporate insurance companies is as communist as it gets? I mean, come on."

The Congresswoman gave an impromptu but impassioned speech upon the bill's arrival. "This is the kind of wasteful spending we see every day from this administration," she shouted, waving the Vice President's Worcestershire-soaked napkin in the air for emphasis. "The American tax-payer should not have to pay for the most irrelevant member of this socialist administration to apply steak sauce, horse-radish, Nutella, and any other condiment he can get his pinko hands on to his medium-rare steak. When will the Democrat party take the deficit seriously?"

Bachman then began chanting, "Make the tax-cuts permanent!" while Biden quietly picked up the bill. At time of printing, FRL was unable to confirm whether the Vice President was able to forge bipartisan compromise in bed.

Assholes delighted
by rise of bathroom graffiti's importance
By Patrick Rooney (FRL!)

Asshole students throughout the UC system are expressing jubilation over bathroom graffiti's increasing prominence as a medium to express their views.

"Our message has long been ignored by the media and the public. People just didn't want to hear what assholes had to say," said Chaz Johnson, a second-year Asshole-American student, as he finished the last of his forty and threw the bottle at a nearby sleeping homeless woman.

"Used to be, I'd draw a swastika on a bathroom wall and people would just scribble it out, or pee on it. Now, it makes headlines and the chancellor emails the whole school to tell them about it."

Sociologist Taylor Wood says the rising popularity of bathroom graffiti has to do with its controversial content, which often consists of "vague ass threats we know they ain't even going to pull off."

Advocacy group Assholes for a Racist Society Everywhere (ARSE) issued a celebratory statement in response.

"For too long, people would sit in a shit-stained public restroom that smelled like some roadkill had been cooked in its own fluids, look over at a misspelled racist screed and think, well this isn't something I need to take seriously. Not anymore! This is a civil rights issue—not the gay kind that helps black people though."

Lady Gaga's "Born this Way" Revolutionizes Catholic Church

"Born this Way," the latest album from pop star/egg creature Lady Gaga has instigated widespread and near total reform of the Catholic Church. The phenomenon is already being described by historians as "as important as Martin Luther's 95 theses, if not more important."

The hubbub began when Cardinal O'Reilly watched the music video "Judas" repeatedly for forty-two hours straight, and then wrote an essay definitively resolving every theological question to have plagued the Church for the past thousand years, including "for how many hours straight must one watch Lady Gaga videos to find the answer to life, the universe, and everything?"

For the Archbishop of Canterbury, the moment of clarity came when he heard Lady Gaga intoning "Jesus is the new black."

"Everything just clicked at that moment," he said. "I was like woah."

The album has also single-handedly transformed the Catholic Church into the gay community's strongest ally. "Gays, lesbians, bisexuals and transsexuals were born that way, just like the Lebanese." declared Pope Benedict XVI to a cheering crowd of thousands dressed in rainbow-colored nun's habits with lobster hats. The infallible leader of the Church added, "I also like the part in the video where Judas pours a beer on Lady Gaga's ass."

After his speech, worshippers turned the Vatican into an enormous dance club, where believers faithfully followed the dictum to "dance dance dance with my hands hands hands above my head like Jesus said."

Meanwhile, Pastor Rick Warren of the Saddleback megachurch has said that he "doesn't really get it," and "she should probably wear more clothes."

And now back to Killing Alaskan Wildlife with Sarah Palin on TLC, The Learning Channel.

[Western style freedom-loving singing:]

> *You need a place to be your sanctuaaary*
> *Where we use guns to kill some stuff*
> *When it cooomes to Sarah Palin*
> *She ain't pulliiing no kind of bluff, no no noooo . . .*

Featuring Sarah Palin and her adorable just-like-you family: Bristol, Todd, Track, Trig, Tractor, Twig, Trigger and Tofu.

Sarah: Today we're going to ride in a helicopter machine over this beautiful God's country and just look around at the beauty that is Alaska. Alaska is the most beautiful, down home regular American place in the world. It's also the biggest place in the world. If you were to walk all the way around Alaska, it would take you nine hundred years and you'd probably miss the second coming of our savior Jesus Christ! Seriously, that's going to happen any day now. And he's going to be really, really peeved at all the abortion and Obamacare that we regular Americans know comes straight from the devil.

Anyway, we're just going to fly around and admire all the beauty. And also we're going to shoot some wolves with machine guns!

I brought along Bristol. She was planning on hanging out with her friends today, but I said, you know, gosh darnit, it'd be really relieving for you just to get away from it all and spend some time with family in the outdoors with lots of video cameras broadcasting to millions on the cable televisions.

Bristol, looking unhappy and speaking robotically: I really wanted to get out and spend time with my mom. My mom is an amazing, independent maverick going rogue. My mom understands that family values are the most important thing which a lot of people maybe in Washington don't understand but I do and she does.

[Aerial shot of mother wolf playing with cubs.]

Sarah: You know, this is just part of the amazing wildlife that we see every day here in Alaska and that I just bet people in big-city fake America don't *ever* see. It's our pleasure just to look at the beautiful animal life and then kill it because that's what real Americans do. A lot of people say that wolves are endangered but those are the some environmentelitists who say that carbon dioxide in the atmosphere somehow makes the earth warmer! I'm like, I'm pretty sure I remember from my schooling that we *breath out* carbon dioxide! And it's still *pretty darn* cold here in Alaska, so what do you say to that? [Chuckles, smiles winningly.]

Anyway, I like to think of it in the way of that old story about little Red State Riding Hood and the wolf that ate all her porridge. Also the wolf is from Kenya, which my advisors tell me is actually *part* of the country of Africa! Who knew, I've never been one of those intellectual eggheads who don't understand real people! I'm all about real Americans and family and that's what I'm all about.

[Stirring music playing over montage of wolf-related carnage.]

Sarah, grinning and shouting over her machine gun: You know, shooting these beautiful creatures just reminds me of one of my favorite sayings in our family: don't retreat, reload. And I try to remember that whether it's moose or mooselims who hate our freedom family liberties.

[Cut to Sarah smiling in front of a pile of wolf corpses and a waterfall of blood.]

Sarah: Doncha know, you gotta drain the wolves first. But it makes me so happy to have this wolf meat for the Christmas season to honor the baby Jesus. All this wolf meat is going in our freezer, and after that it'll make fantastic stocking stuffers!

[Close-up of dead wolves with flies on their eyes.]

Sarah: I just love this hunting stuff because it really weensies up the liberals! And you know, I'm just a Mama Grizzly looking out for her family cubs and you don't wanna mess around with a freedom-loving Alaskan Grizzly!

[Sarah glares at camera.]
[Cut to wolf massacre.]
[Cut to Sarah glaring. Sarah mouths: *Democrats*, and draws a finger across her neck.
[Cut to Todd Palin wringing out blood from a wolf cub.]
[Cut to Sarah Palin, smiling winningly.]
[Credits, music.]

You need a place to be your sanctuaaary
Communists all go to Hell
Don't vote Obaama, don't vote Romney
Vote Sarah Palin Twenty-twelve, oh yeah yeah . . .

NONFICTION

INSIDE KERR HALL

Last night at seven we were expecting the cops to come at any minute. In contrast to the often interminably long meetings that were the norm, we set a limit of half an hour to decide what to do when they arrived. First we voted on whether to put up barricades of some sort besides the ones already behind all entrances to the building besides the front door. The alternative was to leave the front door unblocked, to have a sit-in on the floor and chant when the police came until they physically forced us to leave. It was decided to put up barricades by a slim majority—if I remember correctly, by a vote of 65-68.

I had voted against the barricade. At Berkeley, the occupiers barricaded their building so effectively that a SWAT team had had to break through a window. I imagine this happening on an upper story window, with the SWAT team swinging down on ropes and breaking through with their feet splayed out, but for all I know it was on the first floor and they did it with a hammer. The point is, it seemed to me that we were expecting them to break through and reclaim the building no matter what, so it seemed to me that we might as well do things based on what was best PR. All the same, I hadn't much minded when we decided to put up the barricade; it was a relatively minor issue. By another slim majority, we decided against barricading different floors and moving upstairs to create a kind of fortress.

The plan was to have large numbers of people outside. Some would be there simply to chant and be eyewitnesses when the police came, and others would form a human chain around the building. We would barricade the front door from the inside, which opened out anyway, so it wasn't much of a barricade, and have a sit-in right inside in the front while chanting. There would probably be an opportunity for people who wanted to leave before the final confrontation to do so, and that was fine. It was stressed that those who stayed must act in unity.

Then we played the waiting game. In the meantime, people put together ziplock bags with milk of magnesia-soaked rags inside of them. If you were maced, you were to rub your eyes with the milk of magnesia. There were similar bags with vinegar-soaked rags to breathe through in the event of tear gas, but this was less of a priority. We braced ourselves for anything. At occupations at other campuses, we'd heard of tazing, pepper spray and rubber bullets being used on protesters.

I had an idea that the police would come by midnight, because the negotiators had said something along those lines. When midnight came and went, I began to wonder if they would come at all that night, although I wouldn't have been surprised if they'd come at four in the morning, hoping to catch us all sleeping and less composed. I allowed myself to drink coffee then, which I hadn't before because the last thing I wanted when shit went down was to have to pee.

The tense atmosphere had become more relaxed and fun again. We put on some electronica and danced—well, I didn't dance, but it was still fun. What's that mural on the Merril wall?—*If I can't dance, I want no part in your revolution.* We all felt bad for the people outside in the cold, but all reports said they were having a great time. The press and the faculty who had come at nine had left. I began to wonder if the morning would come and I would just go home and the whole thing would go on without me for another day or more. This is a big reason why the figure of seventy occupiers the administration put out and the press has picked up is such an understatement. There were hundreds of different students who took part in the occupation at different points during the three-day period.

I went to sleep around quarter after four. At five thirty everyone was woken up. "They're coming." I pulled on my shoes, and went blearily to the front entrance. I drank some coke to try to wake up. After a few minutes, somebody asked what exactly prompted them to know the time had come. There were police cars driving all around. This didn't mean the confrontation would happen now, indeed there had been a police presence on campus all night. I went back to sleep.

At seven fifteen we were woken again. "This time it's the real deal." I felt rested, alert. I got my stuff together and went out. My stupid tight jeans had squeezed out most of the milk of magnesia into a dark circle on my thigh. I hoped I wouldn't be maced. I half-hoped I would be arrested.

Going to jail for something I believed in seemed like something cool I could tell my grandkids about. I had mentioned this to my friend Robin the night before. "Yeah," he said, "Going to jail is on this list I saw of five hundred things to do before you die."

The sun hadn't come up yet but it was light outside. My throat burned and I realized I was scared after all.

"Sometimes," I'd told Mr. Weinberger back in high school, "before a performance I'll have this gas, and I'll have to keep burping." That's a problem if you play the trumpet.

He nodded. "I used to have the exact same thing. It's just nerves. It's completely psychological."

I went to the water fountain to quell my completely psychological heartburn, then came back to sit on the floor with everyone.

"Don't take this the wrong way," a guy with a northern European accent said to everyone. "But there is an escape rope out a window in the back if we choose to leave that way."

"No!" we said. "We stick to the plan." But several people left. We'd said all along it was fine for people to leave before the cops broke in, but it still felt odd to see them walk away.

We started singing.

Solidarity forever, solidarity forever, solidarity forever, occupation makes us strong.

The whole thing just took fifteen seconds or so to sing, but we kept repeating it over and over again. Sometimes we changed it up with "education makes us strong."

Just that Friday in my Black Civil Rights class activist photographer Bob Fitch had come to talk to us. Certain things he said kept popping up in my mind, like how when things got tough a song could lift your spirits and keep everyone together. In my limited experience with the protests, we never sang, usually chanting instead, but I was glad we were singing now. We repeated that one verse hundreds of times before it was over. Once somebody tried to start a new song, *Let It Be*. "But we're *not* letting it be!" someone else shouted and that was that, back to Solidarity. At first singing hurt my throat more, but it became something that sustained all of us.

The outside crowd was going wild, jumping and shouting and waving their signs. The cops finally came. There were fifty or so of them in riot gear, and they were an impressive sight in their helmets and clear plastic face shields. In a blue wave they pushed everyone outside to the side with their shields and arms, moving fast. It only took a minute, and then they just milled around outside.

Someone was on the phone with our people outside, and reported to us what was going on. "They've got tear gas canisters and bean bag guns." Someone else was talking to a professor on the phone. She stood up, a very young looking round girl in tie-dye tights. "They're saying that they have to see the barricade as a threat. They say that if we take it down they won't have to resort to violence." She was visibly frightened. "I think we should take it down."

"No!" several people shouted. "What was the point of putting it up, then?"

"Think of your safety!" someone else pleaded. "We should take a vote; things have changed since we voted last night."

Everyone was shouting different things. "Nothing's changed!—No last minute panicked decisions!—They are manipulating you—They are playing on your fear!"

The barricade stayed.

"They're not going to attack us," someone said exasperatedly.

"They're going to rough us up no matter what," someone else said.

I looked at all the cops waiting outside and turned to Robin, sitting next to me. "I feel like we're in a war."

He nodded. "Me too."

Bob Fitch had also talked about gallows humor in civil rights movements. "Maybe by the time this is all over, you'll have some jokes of your own."

A guy with defiant energy radiating from him propped up a little scarecrow Kerr had for autumnal decoration. "The scarecrow will scare the cops away!"

"They're breaking through a barricade in the back," we were informed.

We turned to face the other way, still sitting, still singing. From around the corner we heard breaking and shoving and thudding noises. The two students who were with the press—*The Project* and *City on a Hill*, I think, leveled their cameras at what we couldn't see. Soon they hurried back to us. "It's open." The scarecrow guy had sardonically placed himself in a rolling chair, his arms on the armrests like he was watching a comedy. "Sit on the floor," people yelled to him, and he did.

Still nothing happened. I was ready for them to come in and bash heads if they had to, just get it over with already.

We turned to the front again as two firemen approached the front door. They got the lock open and pulled the door open wide enough to reach in and cut the ties. It only took a minute. The door was open, though there was a thigh-high table-and-fridge barricade they'd have to step over.

The head cop approached us with a couple others. They all wore close-lipped smiles, as though they were trying not to laugh. They looked down at a hundred students or so sitting on the floor, waving peace signs, smiling and singing. He panned a video camera over us slowly, then held out his hands, palms up.

"You sound *beautiful*," he said. "But I just have to read you this." He pulled out a folded sheet of paper. "Your objections have been heard and your point has been made. But you are involved in an illegal operation which has inconvenienced thousands."

We cheered.

"—And you are in violation of California law penal code 602 PC." He paused and waved his hands in the universal *well, come on* gesture. So we cheered at that too. He nodded.

"You have twelve minutes to leave peacefully and orderly through the west entrance to the building. If you do so, no arrests will be made and no charges will be pressed."

"Will there be violence?" the girl in the tie-dye tights asked.

"Violence?" the cop frowned. "No, we just want to get you out of there." He smiled again. "Unless you force our hand."

Twenty people started talking at once. Some were for going right away, others were for staying. I was so committed to the plan that the idea of leaving now seemed bizarre.

"We won," somebody said. "After all that, they're not going to make to press charges? We called their bullshit on the barricades, and they were bluffing. This is the best we'd hoped for."

"That's only a trespassing charge they're saying, too."

Some people got to their feet. "It's individual choice now," they said, though all along we'd stressed the importance of acting in unity.

"What about everyone outside?" someone asked. "They're out there for us."

One of the guys who'd been a sort of leader, though there were no official leaders, said he'd call them. He was muscular and dark-skinned, and it took a while to catch on that he was probably gay.

"Everyone outside wants us to leave safely," he said, and that was that. We all rose and walked around the corner, and out the door, where the path was flanked with twenty more policemen. We flashed the peace sign at them and kept singing.

We reunited with everyone outside in a huge, emotional crowd. Everyone was hugging and crying and laughing, even the professors. "You're amazing," they told us. "No, *you're* amazing," I said to someone who'd stayed the whole night outside. "We did it," people kept saying. "We won. We won."

WHY I OCCUPY

"If you can't explain something simply, you don't understand it."

A week ago I found myself on the roof of a formerly vacant bank building. I was on "cop watch" guard duty, and I won't lie, it was fun.

The Occupy protest movement is going strong after two months at time of writing, but people are still asking, "What are they protesting?" We are protesting economic injustice, in particular that social services are being slashed while the wealthy enjoy record profits, record incomes, and the lowest top income tax rate in half a century.

I'm not a full-time activist or even a particularly shining example of an Occupy participant. I've camped out a couple times, but it's getting cold and I don't predict I'll sleep outdoors again until April or so. I go to marches and general assemblies sometimes, but more often stay home for no better reason than not feeling it. But Occupy excites me, and scathing local media coverage of Occupy Santa Cruz made me feel like explaining myself, for whatever it's worth.

Here's one dude's opinion on what the hell is going on. I think Occupy follows a tradition of leftist organization and protest going back to the Industrial Revolution, when labor exploitation became more . . . efficient. Labor unions and better labor laws won the day after a long, bloody struggle, and continued with the impression that the fight against economic exploitation was not over. Politics in some representative democracies made room for the public display of political vision by making it the platform of an entire party, like Britain's Labour Party. In spite of some effective pressure on electoral politics from Eugene Debs and the Socialist Party, this did not happen with the Democratic or Republican machines.

Flash forward to the 1960s, and please forgive my armchair-historianism. My understanding is that for a long time, the political energy of the left was economic in nature: some were communists, some unionist, but the big theme was a fight against Big Business, who had fought reforms like child labor laws and the minimum wage every step of the way.

But the Vietnam war and the black civil rights movements inspired a New Left generation. They were against segregation and imperialist war, but were mostly middle-class youth whose understanding of unjust economic policy was purely theoretical. Nixon successfully exploited this rift by encouraging blue-collar resentment of college-educated young idealists.

When the Vietnam War ended, the left no longer had an enormous cause to unite them, and split into a million small groups for specific causes—women's liberation, gay rights, environmentalism. In my humble opinion, they're all good causes, but while leftist activists fought the culture war nobly and may have won it, political pressure from corporate America has only grown stronger, and has cememented legislation and policy which redistribute wealth from the working and middle classes to the wealthy.

The Occupy movement has been criticized for its broadness, what Fox News called every liberal cause thrown in a blender. But in its broadness, its commitment to consensus-based decision-making, and its aversion to hierarchical organization, I see a fitting force to the hugeness of the opposition. When the problems faced are so systemic and multi-fronted, how can a movement with any hope of success be anything but broad in nature?

Occupy's broadness means that persons with as different ideologies as libertarianism and Marxism can unite against common causes like the privately-owned Federal Reserve and our system of socialized risk and privatized profit. Occupy's broadness is also at the root of another common criticism: that it has released no formal demands. Some documents like the 99% Declaration have been floating around the internet, with well-articulated demands. But a large portion of members reject any official demands, on the ground that there is nothing to request of a corrupt system short of a different system entirely. Here in Santa Cruz, I went to a "mission statement" workgroup, to participate in hashing out a stated mission to present to the general assembly for approval. My proposal, which I hoped to be broad enough to survive Occupy's process, went like this:

Occupy Santa Cruz exists in solidarity with Occupy Wall Street, a movement against economic injustice.

Corporations are not people. If the Supreme Court insists that they are, under the constitution in its current form, we demand a consitutional amendment to correct this dangerous precedent.

Money does not equal speech. We demand new policy to end the current system of legalized bribery, in which politicians compete for campaign contributions rather than for votes, and reward their corporate pimps once in office.

No more cuts to social services. If they're so concerned about the deficit, let them take it out of the war chest.

My proposal didn't make it out of the work group. One man in particular hated the idea of making any demands, arguing that demands are inherently divisive and therefore unethical and possibly even violent. He is a member of one of the subcultures I've noticed at OSC, which probably exist in other occupations as well. His tribe is the aging hippies, veterans of the sixties, who've come to be part of the new movement. They tend to be "spiritual" and particularly concerned with a nonviolent approach in word and action towards "animal, vegetable and mineral life"—an actual quote. Other tribes include student-activist types, libertarian types, and anarcho-punk types.

I think the uneasiest alliance of all is between those who view Occupy as a protest movement, and those who hope it will be a revolution. Does that sound melodramatic? Not many people I talk to seem to have much faith that American representative democracy is working. People of all political stripes say that the system is broken, so much so that it's common knowledge. If you don't have the money to bankroll your own lobbyist, good luck with your handwritten letter to your congressman. In 2008 we elected a Democratic President and a Democratic super-majority in Congress, only to find that the former opposition party wasn't too interested in changing the status quo. Where does that leave the voter who has only two parties to choose from? If the government has abandoned all pretenses of democracy in favor of legalized bribery and corporatocracy, then the people must find ways outside the system to effect change.

Last week I heard through the grapevine that Occupy Santa Cruz was moving inside, and went to visit the occupied bank I mentioned way at the beginning of this rant. There was some police action, but it was over by the time I got there. Thirty cops in riot gear came, but retreated in the face of a hundred protesters. I'm convinced this is the root of the controversy that 75 River Street became. It deviated from the storyline in which police oust occupations, and many are concerned or even infuriated with police tactics, but in the end order and authority are maintained unchanged. It's more controversial to read on the front page that protesters and police faced off—and the protesters won.

For the indoor occupation to succeed, we needed a level of community support that did not materialize. In fact, even within Occupy Santa Cruz there was controversy over the action, and most full-time occupiers had no interest in leaving San Lorenzo Park. I remember one man who angrily predicted that this would destroy everything we had accomplished. He belongs to an Occupy tribe I failed to mention earlier—the homeless. In Santa Cruz it's illegal to sleep outside within city limits, even in a car. For homeless occupiers, the maintanence of a tent city community is a crucial cause in of itself, rather than a tactic.

The sad truth is that man was mostly right. After the bank occupation, local media like The Santa Cruz Sentinel came down hard on OSC. This was, according to them, an unacceptable escalation and an inexcusable crime, probably even a felony. After a few days of increasing pressure, the occupation ended peacefully. But the police department saw a chance to hit the mother occupation in San Lorenzo Park while public opinion was on their side. It is now mostly dismantled.

If Occupy is a protest movement, it will seek electoral influence. It will send a message to politicians that being the lesser of two evils is no longer enough, and be prepared to "throw votes away" on third-parties to back this up. If Occupy is a nonviolent Egyptian-style revolution, it will become more willing to engage in illegal and controversial acts of civil disobedience. I don't know what will happen, but I'm glad we're trying.

PUBLISHING HISTORY

Leaving the Bungalow was previously published in the 2010 issue of Matchbox Magazine.

Dreamboats was previously published in the 2010 issue of Red Wheelbarrow Magazine.

All *Creative News* articles were originally published by the Fishrap Live!, UC Santa Cruz's premier humor publication, between January and June 2011.

All rights retained by the author.